THE MAGIC SHOP BOOKS
by Bruce Coville

The Monster's Ring
Russell Crannaker, bullied all his life,
gets a chance to fight back when he is given
a monstrous magical item.

Jeremy Thatcher, Dragon Hatcher
Jeremy Thatcher's deepest desires take flight
when he is forced to raise a demanding
dragon hatchling.

Jennifer Murdley's Toad
Jennifer Murdley, a girl "in a plain brown wrapper,"
buys a talking toad who knows a thing or two about
the true nature of beauty.

The Skull of Truth
Charlie Eggleston, who can't help lying,
suddenly must tell the truth and nothing *but* when
he takes the Skull from Mr. Elives' shop.

OTHER BOOKS BY BRUCE COVILLE

The Monsters of Morley Manor

Oddly Enough

Odder Than Ever

Aliens Ate My Homework

My Teacher Is an Alien

Goblins in the Castle

The Dragonslayers

THE UNICORN CHRONICLES

Into the Land of the Unicorns

Song of the Wanderer

Jeremy Thatcher, Dragon Hatcher

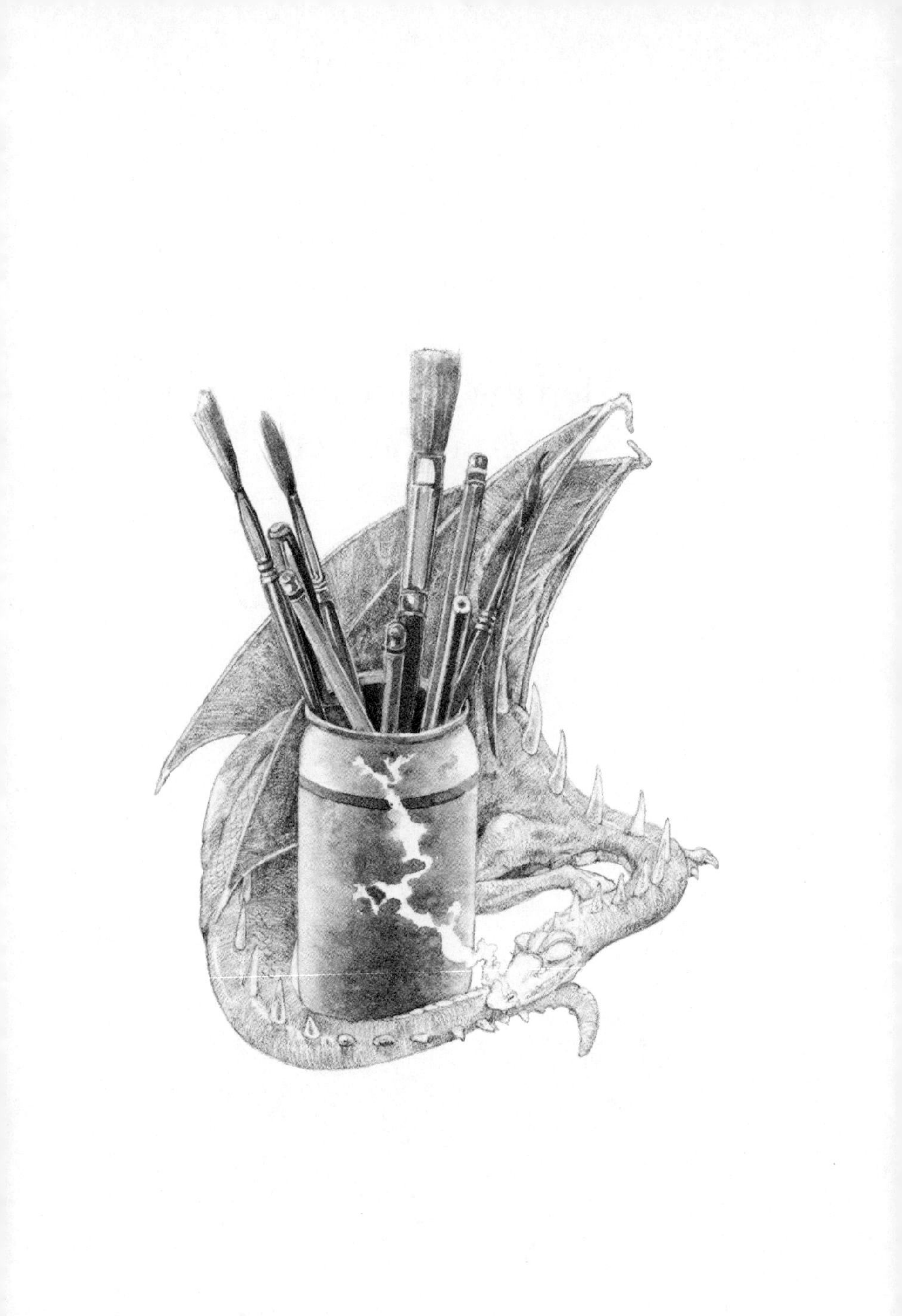

Jeremy Thatcher, Dragon Hatcher

A MAGIC SHOP BOOK

Bruce Coville

ILLUSTRATED BY
GARY A. LIPPINCOTT

HARCOURT, INC.
SAN DIEGO NEW YORK LONDON

www.HarcourtBooks.com

Library of Congress Cataloging-in-Publication Data
Coville, Bruce.
Jeremy Thatcher, dragon hatcher/by Bruce Coville;
illustrated by Gary A. Lippincott.
p. cm.
"A Magic Shop Book."
Summary: Small for his age but artistically talented, twelve-year-old Jeremy Thatcher unknowingly buys a dragon's egg.
[1. Dragons—Fiction. 2. Friendship—Fiction. 3. Pets—Fiction.
4. Drawing—Fiction. 5. Size—Fiction.]
I. Lippincott, Gary A., ill. II. Title.
PZ7.C8344Je 2002
[Fic]—dc20 2002068714
ISBN 0-15-204614-3

Text set in New Baskerville
Designed by Lydia D'moch

A C E G H F D B

Printed in the United States of America

For Jane

Believing in dragons is easy.
Jane believes in people—an act
of love that takes considerably
more imagination.

Contents

ONE

Love Letter of Doom

Jeremy Thatcher crumpled his paper in disgust. The dragon he had been trying to draw looked like a dog with wings.

"Be right back," he whispered to his friend, Specimen. But as he started toward the paper cupboard a sharp voice asked, "Something wrong, Mr. Thatcher?"

Jeremy froze. One of the problems with having Mr. Kravitz for art was that you never knew when it was safe to get a fresh sheet of paper. Clearly, this wasn't one of those days.

The tall, pudgy teacher lumbered over to stand in front of Jeremy. "Didn't you hear the school board has frozen spending?" he asked. "That means no new paper orders for the rest of the year. So tell me, is another sheet of paper needed because that drawing was so bad—or because your talent is so important?"

Mr. Kravitz gave Jeremy a smug, nasty smile and waited for him to answer.

Jeremy hesitated. He wanted to say that his talent *was* that important, but he knew that answer would only bring more scorn. He decided to say nothing. After a moment of uncomfortable silence, he turned and shambled back to his seat.

As Jeremy slid into his chair, Specimen pointed to a square of lavender paper tucked under the corner of Jeremy's books. "From Mary Lou Hutton," he whispered. "Special Delivery."

Jeremy resisted the urge to reach out and grab the note. *No sense in giving Mr. Kravitz something else to complain about,* he thought. *But what am I supposed to do now? My paper is gone, Mr. Kravitz won't let me get more, and I've got fifteen minutes to go before art is over.*

His eyes drifted back to the note. He found himself reaching toward the paper. Quickly, he drew his hand back. *Where's Mr. Kravitz?*

Looking around, Jeremy spotted the art teacher bending over Jymn Magon's desk.

Probably telling him in detail what's wrong with his picture, thought Jeremy. Pretending to look at something else, he tugged the lavender square from its hiding place, unfolded it, and began to read. Before Jeremy could finish, Mr. Kravitz came up and snatched the note from his fingers.

"Well, Mr. Thatcher," he said gleefully. "I see you've forgotten my feeling about notes in the classroom."

Jeremy's cheeks began to burn. "Give it back!" he said.

"I'm afraid I can't do that," replied Mr. Kravitz,

with mock sincerity. "It's against my rules. However, since you didn't have a chance to read it to yourself, I will read it aloud for you before I destroy it."

"Don't!" cried Jeremy in terror.

But Mr. Kravitz had begun. "Dear Jeremy," he read, in mincing tones. "I think you are *incredibly* cute, even if you are the shortest boy in the sixth grade. I am going to kiss you after school today if it's the last thing I ever do."

Mr. Kravitz paused, then said, "Oh, yes—there's a P.S. According to this, you have *beautiful* eyes."

The classroom rocked with laughter. Jeremy closed his "beautiful" eyes, his face so hot that even the tips of his ears were burning.

Mr. Kravitz folded the note and tucked it into his pocket. "No need to embarrass the person who wrote this by reading her signature," he said. "Let's just remember that notes are *not* appreciated in this classroom."

The injustice made Jeremy's head spin. For trying to read a note someone else had given him, he was made to suffer complete humiliation. Yet the person who *sent* the note was getting off with only a warning. What was going on here?

It didn't take him long to figure out the answer. Mary Lou's father was on the school board, so Mr. Kravitz wasn't going to embarrass *her*. Jeremy quivered with the unfairness of it.

"It stinks," he said to Specimen that afternoon. "Stinks, stinks, stinks."

"I agree," said Specimen, pushing up his thick glasses with a long, grubby forefinger. "But then, everyone knows Kravitz hates you."

Jeremy sighed. "All I ever wanted to be is an artist. And the only teacher who's ever really disliked me is my art teacher. I want to know why."

Specimen shrugged. "Forget it. Just be glad he isn't judging the art contest."

Jeremy nodded. He and Spess had been trying to win the spring art contest for years. First prize was the chance to paint the main window of Zambreno's Department Store. Jeremy believed he had had the best entry for the last two years. He hadn't won though, because top spot traditionally went to a sixth grader—whether or not they actually had the best work. Now *he* was a sixth grader, so this should be his year. He was the best artist in the school, and everyone except Mr. Kravitz knew it. The only person who might possibly beat him was Specimen, and they had already decided that whichever one of them won, the other would help with the painting.

However, that didn't take care of his current problem. The fact that everyone in sixth grade knew Mr. Kravitz was a creep had done nothing to protect Jeremy from the teasing that followed the public reading of Mary Lou's love note. Specimen was the only one who had shown him any sympathy. The other boys, particularly Howard Morton and Freddy the Frog Killer, had razzed him unmercifully.

Not that that was anything new.

"Maybe you should just tell everyone who sent the note," suggested Specimen.

"Are you out of your mind?"

Before his friend could answer, Jeremy's stomach lurched with fear. "Spess," he hissed. "It's Mary Lou! She's heading this way!"

"How did she find us?" asked Specimen. "I thought we did a brilliant job sneaking away after school."

Jeremy didn't have time to worry about Mary Lou's tracking abilities. "Just hold her off," he said desperately. Without waiting for an answer, he sprinted away.

"Jeremy Thatcher!" cried Mary Lou. "You get back here!"

Howard Morton and Freddy the Frog Killer were lingering at the end of the block. "Hey, lover boy!" called Howard. "What's the matter? Don't you want your kissy-poo?"

"Shut up, fathead!" yelled Jeremy, as he raced past.

He regretted the words immediately. "Come on, Freddy," yelled Howard. "Let's hold the shrimp down so he can get his kiss!"

Whooping with delight, they joined the chase.

Jeremy pumped his short legs even harder. The thought of Mary Lou's puckering lips gave him new speed. Even so, he could hear Howard and Freddy gaining on him.

Taking a gamble, Jeremy left the sidewalk and began dodging through backyards. He could still hear the voices of his pursuers. Putting on an extra burst of speed, he shot past someone's laundry, down a long driveway, out to a street, then around a corner.

The shrieks and shouts began to fade, but Jeremy ran on until his aching lungs finally forced him to slow to a jog, then a walk. Bending over to hold his throbbing sides, he listened carefully.

Silence!

He stood to look around. A little prickle ran down his spine. *I've never seen this street before.*

That wouldn't have been so strange in a city. But Blodgett's Crossing was a small town.

I've lived here all my life. How can I be lost?

Feeling somewhat nervous, Jeremy followed the street until it came to a tee. He turned right, and entered what began to seem like a maze of unfamiliar streets.

Suddenly he noticed a trace of fog moving around his feet. The afternoon seemed darker than it had just a few moments before.

As he turned in a slow circle, trying to find the way home, he spotted an old-fashioned shop at the end of the street. Its large front window curved out to make a display space. Thin strips of wood divided the window into many small panes of glass. Printed on the window were the words:

ELIVES' MAGIC SUPPLIES
S. H. ELIVES, PROP.

Forgetting his momentary panic, Jeremy walked toward the shop. Who could resist? *Maybe I can find something to make Freddy, Howard, and Mary Lou disappear!* he thought, feeling deliciously cranky.

He didn't really expect that, of course. But he was still excited as he approached the shop.

A large brass knocker hung in the center of the door. Jeremy hesitated. Should he knock?

You don't knock to go into a store, he told himself with a shrug. He pressed on the door. It swung open. A small bell tinkled overhead.

Once inside, Jeremy began to smile. The shop was dark and mysterious. It smelled of some sort of incense—spicy and sharp, yet strangely pleasant.

Magician's equipment crowded the shelves, the display cases, even the floor. A section of one wall was given over to cages filled with rabbits and doves, as well as an odd selection of toads, lizards and—Jeremy squinted to be sure—yes, bats! He walked over to the cages and smiled in approval. The mild, musky smell told him the animals were well cared for.

After a moment he turned from the animals and wandered toward the back of the shop. To his left was a shelf lined with top hats. Chains of jewel-colored silk scarves stretched across the walls and dangled from the ceiling. Directly ahead of him, resting on a pair of dark red sawhorses, was an enormous box made for sawing people in half.

Jeremy spotted an old man—*Mr. Elives?*—pol-

ishing a glass countertop. The man's long white hair hung around his shoulders; his walnut-colored skin had more wrinkles than Jeremy's laundry pile.

Behind the man, a stuffed owl sat on top of the cash register. At least, Jeremy thought the owl was stuffed—until it turned its head, looked directly at him, and began to hoot.

Mr. Elives put down his cloth. "Peace, Uwila," he said. "I know he's here." He turned to Jeremy and frowned, as if the idea of a customer was truly annoying. "Well, what do you want?" he asked sharply.

Jeremy blinked. "I . . . I don't think I want anything," he said. "I just came in to look around."

"No one comes into this shop just to look around," said the old man. "But you can start that way. Let me know when you've found what you need."

Before Jeremy could say that he didn't need anything, the old man picked up his rag and returned his attention to the countertop.

"What an old fruitcake," muttered Jeremy, turning his own attention back to the display cases.

In the first, he found a human skull that looked almost real. "The Skull of Truth," read a hand-lettered label underneath it. Next to the skull was a collection of Chinese rings. And next to the rings, resting on a kind of pedestal, was a shining, multicolored ball, almost the size of his fist. A thousand different hues seemed to shimmer across its glistening surface. Jeremy turned his head slightly and the colors shifted into a new pattern. He blinked and looked more closely. The colors were moving on their own.

"How much does this cost?" he asked.

Mr. Elives glanced up from his work. "You don't want that."

"How do you know whether I want it?"

"That's my business."

Jeremy wasn't sure if the old man meant knowing that sort of thing *was* his business, or if he was just saying not to be nosey.

Whatever he meant, he was wrong. Jeremy *did* want the beautiful, ever-changing sphere.

"How much is it?" he asked again.

Mr. Elives sighed and shuffled over to the display case. "Do you have any idea what this is?"

Jeremy shrugged. "Some kind of marble?"

"Don't be a fool. Look at it again."

Jeremy stared at the strange sphere. "All right, it's too big for a marble. What is it?"

"Never mind."

Jeremy swallowed. This old guy was even crazier than he looked. If he hadn't wanted to know more about the ball he might have fled the shop right then. Turning his attention back to the display case, he said, "Can I see it?"

"You're seeing it right now."

Jeremy barely stopped himself from being truly rude. "I mean," he said carefully, "may I look at it more closely?"

The old man hesitated. After a moment he knelt and opened a wooden drawer at the bottom of the cabinet. It was filled with boxes of all sizes and colors. The old man chose one lined with soft cotton.

Next he reached into his pocket and pulled out an enormous set of keys. He searched through them, muttering to himself, until he found the one he wanted. It was long and black. Unlocking the glass door on the front of the case, he slid it to the right, reached in and picked up the ball. Placing it gently in the box, he stood and put the box on the counter.

Jeremy swallowed nervously. Something strange seemed to be happening inside him. "It's beautiful," he whispered, reaching out to pick it up.

The old man moved as if to stop him, then dropped his hand and shrugged.

Jeremy lifted the sphere out of the cotton and smiled. It felt warm and comfortable in his hand. He wanted it more than ever.

The old man blinked. A puzzled expression wrinkled across his face. Muttering to himself, he reached out, took the ball from Jeremy, and stared at it. For a moment he seemed worried. Then he sighed and shook his head.

"Do you have a quarter?" he asked.

"What?"

"I said, do you have a quarter? You may have it for a quarter."

Jeremy looked up in surprise. "I thought you said I didn't want it."

The old man looked directly into Jeremy's eyes. "You don't," he said softly. "*It* wants you."

TWO

Strange Instructions

Jeremy wondered if the old man really was out of his mind.

"A quarter," said Mr. Elives again, holding out his hand.

Jeremy fumbled in his pocket; he wasn't sure he had a quarter. He wondered if the old man would accept two dimes and a nickel instead. Mr. Elives was so weird it was hard to tell.

The old man frowned.

Jeremy felt both relieved and frightened when his fingers finally closed on a quarter. "Here," he said nervously, holding up the coin.

Mr. Elives snatched it away. "Stand still," he said. "I have to get something."

Jeremy stood. In fact, he felt as if his feet had been frozen to the floor. He had no idea how much time went by before the old man returned carrying a yellowed piece of paper, which he folded into a square, then tucked into the box next to the sphere.

He handed the box to Jeremy. Then he reached forward, grabbed him by the shoulders, and looked straight into his eyes. After only a few seconds Jeremy wanted to break the stare-down. To his horror, his eyes seemed to be locked in place. No matter how he struggled, he couldn't look away.

"Follow the instructions exactly," whispered the old man. "And for Ishtar's sake, be careful. If you fail to care for this properly, you will have *me* to answer to!"

Then, as if the whole situation were an annoyance he wanted to be done with, he snapped, "Take the side door. It will get you home faster."

Clutching the box, Jeremy ran out the door. When he stopped to look around, he found himself on Maple Street, not far from his house.

Now how did I get here?

For the life of him, he could *not* remember. One minute he had been in that weird shop. The next—here he was, less than a block from home.

At least he was safe. Howard and Freddy rarely came this far from the center of town. Of course, living out here meant Jeremy had to walk farther to get to school than most of his friends. But the fact that he had a backyard that was more like a back field made up for it. The place had been a working farm once and his father, who was a veterinarian, used the main barn as an office.

Jeremy tucked the box under his arm. Watching carefully for Howard, Freddy, or Mary Lou, he crossed the street and headed for his front door.

When he entered the house, he was nearly overwhelmed by Grief—which was what his family called their golden retriever. The bounding dog greeted him with an explosion of enthusiasm that almost knocked the box out of his hand.

"Down, Grief!" he yelled, as he battled his way past the big dog's thumping goodwill. "DOWN!"

Grief paid no attention. But then, he never did.

Jeremy sighed. His parents had a small kid—why couldn't they have a small dog? Holding the box over his head, he finally managed to put it safely on top of the piano. Then he led the bouncing dog to the kitchen, which, as usual, was occupied by a surprising number of cats.

Sliding one of the cats away from the pantry door, Jeremy found a chew-bone. He tossed it to Grief, who ran off, growling happily.

Retrieving the box, Jeremy headed up the stairs. A pile of clean clothes blocked his doorway. His mother had been leaving his laundry outside his door ever since the morning three months ago when she had stepped in a vat of papier-mâché that was sitting in front of his dresser.

"Driving to work every day is dangerous enough," she had told Jeremy that night. "I don't need to try to survive crossing your floor, too."

He stepped over the laundry and closed the door behind him. Though he was eager to examine the sphere and the paper the old man had given him, a chorus of eager squeaks told Jeremy that his animals wanted to be fed.

With a sigh, he placed the box on his desk and started the rounds of his room. Peering into each of the dozen or so small cages that lined the shelves and walls, he made sure that the mice, gerbils, hamsters, and guinea pigs all had food and water. The guinea pigs, who already had plenty of food, wouldn't stop shrieking until he gave them more.

Animals fed, Jeremy sat down to study the ball. Shoving aside a stack of unfinished drawings, he placed the box in the center of his desk and took off the lid.

It's like a kaleidoscope, he thought, as the colors swirled in the light of his desk lamp. *Except you don't need to look through a tube to see it.*

Marveling that the old man had sold him such a wonder for only a quarter, Jeremy reached out to touch its glossy surface. With a cry of surprise he pulled back his hand.

The ball was warmer than before. Eying it nervously, Jeremy unfolded the paper the old man had tucked into the box. *Probably directions for keeping it clean,* he thought, as he spread the paper out on his desk. But when he looked at it, he blinked in surprise.

A picture of a dragon stretched up the left side and around the top corner of the page. A burst of flames extending from its mouth separated into fiery letters that said, "How to Hatch a Dragon's Egg."

Jeremy frowned. *What kind of fool does that old man think I am?*

The whole thing was ridiculous. But it was also

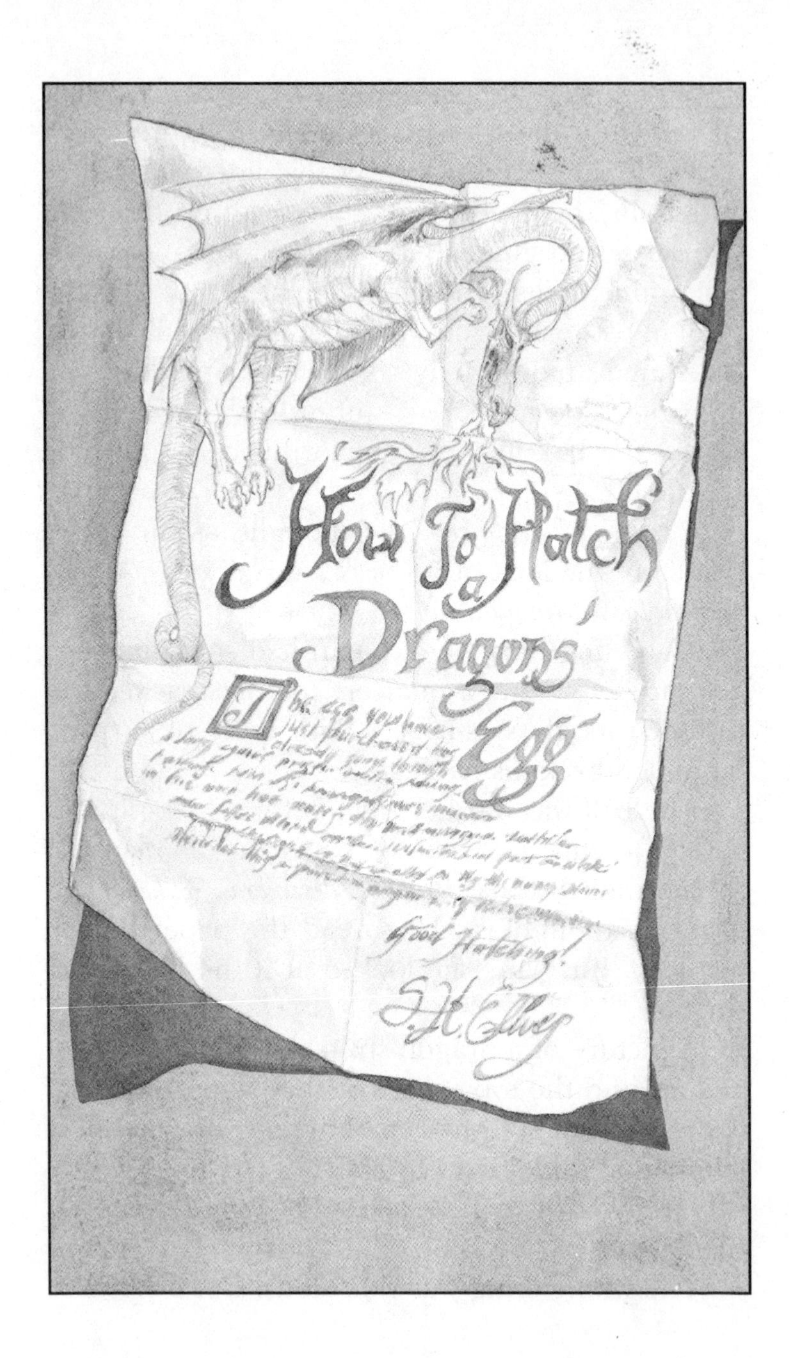
How To Hatch a Dragon's Egg
Good Hatching!

intriguing, so he decided to read the rest of the page, which had been written by hand in a script that was loose and spidery.

How to Hatch a Dragon's Egg

The egg you have just purchased has already gone through a long aging process. It now needs but two things to be ready to hatch—the light of a full moon, and the words of a true friend.

To quicken the egg, take it outside at midnight on the night of the next full moon. Lift it to the moonlight and whisper:

Full moon's light to wake the egg,
Full moon's light to hatch it;
Midsummer Night will crack the world,
But St. John's Day will patch it.

Expose the egg to the moonlight for at least three hours, then await the results.

You have been entrusted with a very special creature, Jeremy Thatcher. Treat it with care, for its safety depends upon your willingness to follow these directions exactly.

It goes without saying that secrecy is essential.

Good hatching!

—S. H. Elives

Jeremy felt the hairs at the back of his neck begin to prickle. *How did that old man know my name?*

he wondered. He was sure he had never mentioned it.

"Hey, Bub!" said a voice, making him jump.

The voice came from a speaker mounted on the wall next to his desk—part of the intercom system his dad had installed during the last burst of what Jeremy's mother called "Herbert's occasional electronic enthusiasms."

"Hey, Bub," repeated his father. "Are you there?"

"I'm here," said Jeremy, somewhat reluctantly.

"Well, you shouldn't be. You should be *here,* getting your chores done."

Despite the admonishing words, Dr. Thatcher's voice was cheerful.

"Be right there," said Jeremy, trying to sound enthusiastic.

Slipping the instructions under a pile of his drawings, Jeremy headed out of his room and down the stairs. With Grief bouncing at his heels, he ambled down the winding driveway, past the pair of small barns, to his father's veterinary office. Stepping inside, Jeremy found his father shoving vitamins into a ferret.

"Hold still, ho-o-old still," crooned Herbert Thatcher to the squirming mass of brown and yellow fur in his hands. "Ah, there's a love!"

Jeremy reached out to take the ferret.

"Hey, kiddo," said his father, handing over the animal. "How was your day?"

Jeremy put the ferret on his shoulder. The action gave him a chance to think about his father's question.

"Complicated," he said at last, squirming a bit as the little animal licked his ear.

Dr. Thatcher raised an eyebrow, his way of requesting more information.

"Well, for one thing, Mary Lou Hutton wants to kiss me."

Dr. Thatcher wrinkled his nose. "That's what you get for being so cute."

"I'm not cute!"

"Okay, you're ugly. Put Farrah in her cage and go feed the cats. I've got one more patient to see before I can knock off for the night."

Jeremy caged the ferret, then found the cat food and began filling the dishes. In the next to last cage crouched an enormous orange-and-white cat with tattered ears and a swollen eye.

"Hey, Pete," said Jeremy. "How ya doin'?"

The cat—whose full name, according to his owner, was "Fat Pete, *Porkus Extremus*"—was in the office at least once a month to get stitched up after one of his fights. While today's eye problem was new, the tattered ears had been that way for years.

Jeremy reached through the bars to scratch behind Pete's ears. The cat responded by clawing his hand.

Jeremy pulled back. "Why, you rotten . . ."

"Jeremy!" called his father from the other room. "What's the rule?"

Jeremy sighed. "There's no sense in getting mad

at a cat for being a cat." He knew it was true, but he stuck his tongue out at Pete anyway.

After all the animals were fed, Jeremy and his father walked back to the house. The sky was dark with clouds, and in the distance they could hear a rumble of thunder.

"When's the next full moon?" Jeremy asked suddenly, as they reached the back door.

Dr. Thatcher, who was apt to burst into song whenever something reminded him of a lyric, threw back his head and sang, "Full mooooon brings empty heart—"

"Dad!"

Dr. Thatcher paused. "I don't know," he said. "But it can't be long. Go get today's paper."

"I don't think a full moon counts as big news, Dad."

"Just get the paper."

Jeremy got the paper. His father showed him the almanac on the inside of the first page. It told when the sun came up, when it was going to set, what time the moon rose and set, and other equally trivial things.

"They're not so trivial when you want to know them," said Dr. Thatcher. "Anyway," he continued, pointing to the almanac, "to answer your question, the next full moon is tonight."

"Tonight!"

Dr. Thatcher glanced at his watch. "Starting in about two hours," he said. "Assuming it doesn't rain."

Jeremy swallowed. He didn't really believe the thing upstairs was an egg. But if he wanted to know for sure, he'd have to start tonight. Either that, or wait another whole month.

Leaving his father, he went upstairs to look at the ball. He picked it up and held it for a moment. It was warmer than ever. Pulling out the directions, he made up his mind.

Tonight he would try to hatch a dragon.

THREE

Hatchling

Jeremy stared in misery at the rain pounding against his window. A streak of lightning sizzled through the dark sky. Seconds later a roof-shaking clap of thunder made Grief jump onto Jeremy's bed and start to whine.

Jeremy felt like whining, too. Though he was far from convinced that the thing he had bought in the magic shop was really an egg, he was still nervous. The directions said to expose it to the *next* full moon.

"But what—" he whispered to the window, "what if the next full moon never shows up?"

His worries were balanced by the feeling that the whole thing was nothing but a hoax—a joke being played by a weird old man with a warped sense of humor. Even so, Jeremy whispered the hatching poem to himself as he crawled into bed, repeating it until he was sure he had it memorized.

"Full moon's light to wake the egg," he was saying when he heard his parents' footsteps on the stairs. "Full moon's light to hatch—"

He fell silent as a crack of light appeared at the door. It was his mother, peeking in to see if he was all right.

"Good night, sweetheart," she whispered, as she did every night, thinking that he was asleep and could not hear her.

The house settled down, but Jeremy couldn't. Sounds drifted through the darkness: a cat bounding across the kitchen, the squeak of exercise wheels as his pets raced in place through the night, the patter of rain at the windows, the occasional sizzle-boom of lightning followed by thunder.

And then, at five minutes to midnight, silence.

Jeremy sat up in bed. The rain had ended as suddenly as it had begun. Moonlight was flooding through his window.

Breathing softly, not moving, Jeremy listened. When he was satisfied that the house was completely silent, he climbed out of bed, slipped into his clothes, and picked up the bag he had packed earlier. It contained the egg (still in its box), a towel, and a small windup clock.

Feeling slightly foolish, he tiptoed down the stairs. The kitchen cats twined around his feet, begging for a snack. Ignoring them, Jeremy slipped out the back door.

The night air smelled of the rain. The wet grass, a little long because—despite his promise—Jeremy had not mowed yet this week, sparkled in the moonlight.

A huge moon floated above the treetops. In its light, the whole world seemed to be made of black and silver.

The high, frantic chorus of the spring peepers almost covered the sound of the wind as it moved through the newly opened willow leaves.

Jeremy's heart pounded wildly with the sense of magic flooding the night.

By the time he found a place he thought would be free of shadows for the next three hours, the grass had soaked his legs all the way to the calves.

Hoping that neither of his parents would happen to wake and look out their window, he took the egg from its box, lifted it toward the dazzling moon, and repeated the poem he had memorized earlier:

> Full moon's light to wake the egg,
> Full moon's light to hatch it;
> Midsummer Night will crack the world,
> But St. John's Day will patch it.

A tendril of gold light trickled through Jeremy's mind, making him shiver.

What was that?

Shaking his head, he took out the towel and spread it on the grass with his free hand. Then he placed the egg on top of it. Next, he twisted the key in the back of the little clock, and set it to ring at exactly 3:15 A.M.

Now everything was ready except Jeremy himself. After a few minutes of standing ankle deep in the wet grass, looking at the egg, and listening to the peepers, he pulled one of his mother's reclining lawn chairs over to the towel. He shook as much water off it as he could, then settled down to watch over the egg.

Lying on his back, he could see the dark forms of bats flapping their way through the lesser darkness of the night. Beyond the bats lay the stars. He began to look for constellations. As he was picking out Draco, the great dragon that twisted between the Dippers, he drifted off to sleep.

In his dreams, Jeremy ran from Mary Lou Hutton. But no matter how desperately he pumped his legs, his body wouldn't move. Mary Lou kept getting closer and closer, her giant lips smacking with the kiss of death. She was about to grab him when the clock began to jangle. Jeremy slammed off the alarm automatically. Then he opened his eyes and sat up with a shout.

The moonlight dazzled and confused him. "Where am I?" he whispered.

When he finally remembered why he was outside, he turned to the egg and blinked in surprise. While the shifting of hues had been slow and subtle before, the colors were now swirling across the egg in a way that should have been impossible.

He picked it up in awe. What was he supposed to do now?

Wait, according to the directions.

But how long?

As if in answer, the egg shook in his hands. The dancing colors froze in place. He heard a scratching sound. Suddenly a single, sharp claw pierced the shell. The tiny talon sparkled like a jewel in the moonlight.

Jeremy cried out. His first instinct was to drop the egg—maybe even throw it. Taking a deep breath, he forced his hands to stay steady.

Moving slowly, he bent to put the egg on the lawn. But when his fingers brushed the soaking grass he stopped. "Maybe I shouldn't get you wet," he whispered.

Standing again, he held the egg in front of him. He wondered if he should take it inside. After all, the old man had told him to care for it, and if it hatched out here, he might lose whatever was hatching.

But maybe I'm supposed to lose it, he thought, feeling fairly certain that whatever was coming out of the egg wasn't the kind of thing one would keep for a pet. *I sure don't want to go inside with something that's going to have us for supper.*

Yet whatever was in the egg couldn't be very big. Somehow it didn't seem right to leave a baby out here to fend for itself.

"Inside it is!" he said aloud. As he began to run toward the back door, shining chips of shell fell into his cupped hands. "Hold on," he whispered, as another claw appeared. "Just hold on. We're almost there."

Shifting the egg so that he could carry it in one hand, he opened the door as quietly as possible. Entering on tiptoe, he eased the door shut behind him. A kitchen cat stared defiantly from the forbidden counter; Grief was nowhere in sight. Still on tiptoe, Jeremy climbed the stairs, the egg twitching and jerking in his hand.

In his bedroom, he placed the egg gently on his desk. Then he crossed the room and turned the bedside lamp on low. Returning to his chair, he watched in fascination as the gleaming, diamond-like claws continued to chip away at the shell.

Suddenly a scaly red arm stretched into the light. Now the hole in the egg began to grow faster. Within seconds, the head appeared.

Jeremy gasped. Despite everything that had gone on, despite the magic shop and all its strangeness, in his heart he had never really believed that what was inside the egg was anything more exotic than a lizard. But with its plated chest and winged shoulders, the creature that now emerged from the shell could only be one thing. It could only be a dragon.

The wings hung limp and crumpled at the dragon's side. At first Jeremy was afraid something was wrong with the animal. But then it started to twitch its shoulders. Soon the wings began to lift and fill. Except for the fact that they were bright

red, they looked a great deal like a bat's wings. When they were finally fully extended Jeremy felt a surge of triumph so strong it was almost as if he had managed to pump up the wings himself.

The little dragon looked around, sniffed, then began crawling across the desk. Jeremy pulled back nervously. Holding his breath, ready to run if necessary, he watched in wonder. Something began to tickle at the back of his mind. He stared at the dragon, and it locked eyes with him.

For a moment, Jeremy felt as if he were drowning in green. Then the baby curled up, dropped its head over its tail, and closed its eyes.

The green disappeared.

Jeremy felt exhausted. But he was also beginning to feel a little safer. Curled up, the dragon was no bigger than a medium-sized grapefruit, and about as threatening. Jeremy found himself longing to touch the gleaming red scales. After the beast's eyes had been closed for several minutes, he put out a tentative finger to stroke its head.

The dragon opened its eyes and reared back, hissing ferociously. A slender red tongue flickered over the tiny fangs, reminding Jeremy of the lightning that had split the sky earlier that night. He sat in frozen terror. The dragon hissed again, then arched its back, stretching its leathery red wings into the air.

For a long moment boy and beast stared at each other. Suddenly colors began to swirl in Jeremy's head, almost as if he were looking at the egg again.

Moving slowly, the dragon resumed its curled position. But this time it did not close its eyes. It simply lay on the desk staring at him. Once it sniffed, sending a tiny puff of smoke out of its nostrils.

Jeremy took advantage of the truce to study the beast. In the low light of the lamp its burnished scales shone like polished copper. The glittering green eyes, examining Jeremy as carefully as he was examining their owner, looked like a pair of intelligent emeralds. Each of its feet had four toes. From the tip of each toe stretched a tiny claw that looked like a chip of cut diamond. A ridge of pointed plates, none more than a quarter of an inch high, ran from the top of the dragon's head to the tip of its tail.

After a few minutes, the dragon lifted its head and made a tiny snuffling noise. Then it asked Jeremy a question.

Jeremy had no idea what the question was. But he could feel the question-*ness* of it inside his head, almost as if the dragon were using its ferocious little claws to etch a question mark into his brain.

But nothing about the question itself was ferocious. It was simply that: a question. Sensing the little creature's genuine puzzlement, Jeremy's feelings shifted from awe to protectiveness. He put his hand forward again.

This time the hatchling didn't move.

Holding his breath, Jeremy inched his hand even

closer. When the dragon still didn't move, he cocked out one finger.

The dragon darted forward and nipped his fingertip.

"Ow!" cried Jeremy, pulling back his hand. "You rotten—"

His burst of anger was cut off by a wave of puzzled sorrow that started in the back of his head and shivered all the way through his body.

Jeremy looked at his fingertip. Though a half-circle of red dents ringed the fleshy side, the skin was unbroken.

"Are you trying to play?"

Moving cautiously, he extended his hand again.

The dragon stretched its neck forward. This time it moved as slowly as the boy. Opening its jaws, it took Jeremy's fingertip delicately between its teeth, then shook its head gently from side to side before letting go.

"Almost like shaking hands," said Jeremy softly. Feeling braver, he reached forward and stroked the dragon's thumb-sized head. The dragon closed its eyes and made a little chittering noise.

Jeremy smiled.

He had just made friends with a dragon!

Dawn found Jeremy still at his desk, the dragon perched on his shoulder, nibbling contentedly, but ineffectively, at his ear. As Jeremy watched the sun rise, he decided it was a good thing the dragon had hatched on a Friday night. He had a lot to do before he could go off and leave it on its own all day. First and foremost, he had to figure out what to feed it. In the stories he remembered, dragons dined on fair young maidens. All in all, that seemed like a bad idea.

Jeremy rummaged through the stack of drawings where he had hidden the instruction sheet. Maybe it held some information he had overlooked.

When he finally found it, he felt such a jolt of surprise that he cried out as if the paper had burned him.

FOUR

Hyacinth Priest

Jeremy stared at the direction sheet. The top of the page had changed. Where it had once read, "How to Hatch a Dragon's Egg," it now said, "The Care and Feeding of Dragons."

When had it changed? And *how?*

Fingers trembling, he picked up the paper. The dragon tickled his ear with its tongue as he began to read.

THE CARE AND FEEDING OF DRAGONS

You have been chosen to care for a rare and precious creature, Jeremy Thatcher. When fully grown, your dragon will be unimaginably powerful. But in the early stages of its development, it is very vulnerable. Like any infant, it must be cared for if it is to survive.

To begin with, you must guard the fact of its existence. The world at large does not love dragons. Should your dragon be discovered, it will almost certainly be taken from you.

As to feeding: while mature dragons prefer live food, an infant will be satisfied with something that has already been killed. Small gobbets of meat, such as chicken livers, are particularly appropriate. When the dragon is older, it will be able to hunt for itself. (Dragons grow rapidly, so you will need to think about protecting your pets before long.)

Eventually your dragon will shed its skin. Do not be alarmed by this. However, you must save the skin, as well as the baby teeth, which will begin to fall out at about the same time. You must also save as much of the eggshell as possible. These things will be very important when Midsummer Night arrives.

Your dragon must have a name. Actually, every dragon is born with a name. However, since these birth names must remain secret, you should provide another name as soon as possible.

Finally—your dragon will be very sensitive to your own emotional state. It would be wise to avoid extreme agitation while raising the dragon. If you do not, trouble may result.

It's a good thing Mom and Dad sleep late on Saturdays, thought Jeremy as he tiptoed into the kitchen. Opening the refrigerator, he stared inside. Suddenly he became aware of something big and furry standing next to him.

"Grief!" he whispered. "Get out of here!"

The golden retriever looked up at him with a wounded expression. However, if the dog was wounded, he was not offended enough to leave. Leaning against Jeremy, he stared into the refrigerator.

Boy and dog moved their heads in unison as they scanned the lower shelves, which were filled with plastic containers. Jeremy knew that most of them held stuff like leftover rice pudding. But he knew, too, that there must be some chicken livers here. His father ate them all the time.

Gathering his courage, he pulled open the meat tray.

There they were! Jeremy shivered as he pulled the container out of the fridge.

"Gross," he moaned when he opened it and actually saw the chunks of slippery purple meat. *How can Dad even touch these things,* he thought, *much less* eat *them?*

His revulsion was multiplied when he felt something wet on his bare foot and looked down to find that Grief was drooling on him.

Jeremy shook his foot. The glob of slobber spread out a bit, but otherwise stayed in place. He pulled a paper towel from the roll sitting on the counter and bent down to wipe away the dog spit.

"You make me sick!" he hissed at Grief.

The dog licked his face.

Totally disgusted, Jeremy pulled one of the chicken livers out of the container and threw it across the room. Grief ran after it with such lust that he smashed into a cupboard.

"What's going on down there?"

Jeremy flinched. "Just giving Grief his breakfast, Dad!" he yelled, hoping his father would be too groggy to remember that it had been months since he had voluntarily fed the dog.

"Well, do it a little more quietly!" shouted Dr. Thatcher. "Some people are still sleeping around here."

"Okay, Dad. Sorry about that."

Jeremy waited, but there were no more words from upstairs. He relaxed. His father must have collapsed back into sleep.

Walking on tiptoe, he led Grief outside and clipped his collar to the chain attached to the corner of the garage. He slipped back inside, gently pulling the door closed behind him.

That was better. He would never get these stupid things upstairs with Grief around.

Back at the counter, Jeremy pulled out two more livers. *Uck! They feel as bad as they look.*

Quivering with disgust, he dropped the cold meat onto a saucer, then put the container back into the fridge. Picking his way through the cats, he shut the kitchen door and started up the stairs.

When he entered his room, the dragon was nowhere to be seen. *Where did it go?* he thought desperately.

As he was heading for his desk he heard a soft hissing. Looking up, he saw the dragon swooping toward him, its pointy red wings stretched to the full.

"Yow!" cried Jeremy, jumping back.

The dragon landed on the edge of the saucer and began to nip at one of the livers.

Jeremy held the saucer at arm's length. "You," he said to the dragon, "are a troublemaker. *And* you have bad taste."

But as he set the saucer down—with the dragonlet still clinging to the edge—Jeremy again found himself entranced by the strange beauty of the little beast.

When the dragon was done eating, it walked across the desk and began to climb Jeremy's arm. Its tiny claws felt like needles against his skin.

"Ouch!" cried Jeremy. "Cut that out!"

The dragon ignored his protest. It continued up his arm until it reached his shoulder, where it settled down with a little sigh that sent a puff of hot air across his cheek.

Jeremy slid the saucer aside and pulled the instruction sheet out of the desk drawer.

"Your dragon must have a name," he read aloud. He reached up to pat the little animal, which had curled up on his shoulder. "What about it, beastie?" he asked softly. "What should we call you?"

To his surprise, the dragon answered him.

The answer did not come in words. It came as a feeling of *not knowing* that reminded Jeremy of the blank sensation he got whenever Mr. Sigel called on him in math.

He turned his head and looked at the dragon out of the corner of his eyes. It yawned, opening its mouth so wide that Jeremy could no longer see the jewellike eyes.

Jeremy laughed. It had never occurred to him that a dragon could be cute. But this one certainly was. At least, it was now. He wasn't sure what it would be like when it got bigger. Maybe being small made things cute.

"I suppose that's true," he said out loud, thinking of the women who were always coming up to pinch him on the cheek and tell him how cute he was. As if being cute were something wonderful. Personally, he hated being cute—*and* being small.

"At least *you'll* grow out of it," he said to the dragon.

He thought about that for a second. The dragon might stop being cute *fast* once it started to grow. The idea was frightening. Just how big was this thing going to get?

Other than mentioning that it would be large enough to eat the family pets, the "Care and Feeding" sheet wasn't very specific about growth. Nothing it said indicated the *upper* limit of the dragon's size. Would it get to be as big as a car? A bus? A house?

It was time to do some research.

Since Jeremy's bike was broken, he had to go to the library on foot. The head librarian was just taking down the CLOSED sign when he arrived, puffing with exhaustion from having run all the way.

She took one look at him and said, "Overdue homework, Jeremy?"

He shook his head. "I just need to find out some stuff," he gasped.

"It's wonderful to see someone so hungry for knowledge," she replied, sounding as if she didn't quite believe him.

Jeremy gave her a fake smile and headed for the back of the library. His smile became real when he saw the long-haired children's librarian. She was sitting at her desk and staring at a book with a look of fierce concentration. The sign in front of her said: MISS HYACINTH PRIEST.

Jeremy crossed the room quietly and stood by Miss Priest's desk. After a moment she looked up.

"Good morning, Jeremy," she said. Her voice had a hint of music to it, and he always liked to hear her talk. "Have you come for some more art books?"

He shook his head. "New topic today. I need to find out about dragons."

Miss Priest looked at him carefully. "Fascinating creatures," she said at last. "Let's see what we can dig up."

She stood, towering over Jeremy, and led him past rows of books, until they came to the section she was looking for. She bent forward to scan the shelves, causing the blue beads of her long, dangling earrings to brush the sides of her face.

"Aha!" she said, reaching out to snatch up a thin volume. "I thought you might be hiding here."

Without looking up, she handed the book to Jeremy. "Now, where's your friend?" she muttered.

"Spess doesn't do libraries," said Jeremy, before he realized she had been addressing the book.

Suddenly her hand darted forward again. "Here we go!" she said triumphantly.

She handed Jeremy a medium-sized book. A wonderful red dragon reared across the green cover, its claws outstretched, a shaft of flame rocketing from its mouth. Jeremy wished desperately that he could draw like that.

Ten minutes later Jeremy was sitting at a long wooden table with a thick stack of books beside him. He opened the first and started looking for something—anything—that would tell him what to do with a dragon.

He had no idea how long he had been reading when his concentration was interrupted by a pang of hunger shooting through his stomach.

He closed the book and rubbed his belly.

How long has it been since I ate?

Glancing at the clock on the wall, he was surprised to see that it was only 10:15.

He decided to read a little longer. He was enjoying the books, even if they didn't provide much useful information. The only problem was that in almost every story the dragon got killed at the end—

usually with good reason, since most of them were extremely nasty. About the only good dragons he had found were Chinese.

He wondered if dragons were really that terrible, or if people just said bad things about them because they *looked* so scary.

More to the point, what was *his* dragon going to be like?

Opening the green book, Jeremy found a story about a dragon named Niddhogg. He wrote the name on his notepad. The list of possible dragon names was about the only real stuff he had gotten so far.

He had barely finished writing *Niddhogg* when the next hunger pang hit. His stomach began to rumble threateningly. Gathering the books he wanted to check out, he took them to Miss Priest.

"Did you find what you were looking for?" she asked.

"Not everything," he admitted.

Hyacinth Priest paused, then leaned toward him and said softly, "Just exactly what *are* you looking for?"

Jeremy swallowed. "This is going to sound silly," he began. Before he could finish, his stomach began making a noise like an erupting volcano.

Miss Priest nodded. "Very silly," she said seriously.

Jeremy blushed. "I mean my question will sound silly."

The librarian looked directly into his eyes. "No

question is silly if you really want to know the answer," she said fiercely.

"Okay," said Jeremy. "Then what I want to know is, do you have anything on how to *raise* a dragon?"

Miss Priest smiled. "Of course," she said softly.

FIVE

Things Unseen

The book Miss Priest pulled from the bottom drawer of her desk felt as if it had been bound with real leather. The cover had no words on it, not even a title. Ignoring the crescendo of his stomach symphony, Jeremy opened it.

The first page was as blank as the cover. On the second page, however, he found the title, *On the Nature (and Disappearance) of Dragons.*

Jeremy turned the page again, and nearly dropped the book. In addition to the title, this page added the name of the author: S. H. Elives.

Jeremy's skin began to prickle. He looked at Miss Priest. "Where did you get this?"

Hyacinth Priest shrugged. "Who knows where books come from? It's really a very great mystery, isn't it?"

"Can I check it out?"

Miss Priest nodded. "I've been saving it for you."

The little hairs on the back of Jeremy's neck

began to bristle. "How did you know I would be wanting it?"

Miss Priest raised an eyebrow. "What are librarians for?" she asked. She reached forward and took Jeremy's wrist. Looking straight into his eyes, she said, "I would read that book very carefully if I were you, Jeremy Thatcher. Very carefully indeed."

Jeremy spent most of the walk back to his house thinking alternately about his conversation with Miss Priest and about how incredibly hungry he was.

He had almost made it through the park when a familiar voice called, "Jeremy! Hey, Jeremy!"

He said a bad word. Mary Lou Hutton was the last thing he needed right now. "I should have known better than to walk home this way," he muttered.

He considered running, but with the load he was carrying, he didn't have a chance of escaping.

"How come you have so many books?" asked Mary Lou, falling into step beside him. "I didn't know you liked to read."

Jeremy stopped and turned to her. "What do you think?" he asked angrily. "Only girls like to read? I read lots."

"Like what?"

Jeremy wanted to tell her to go away. But he knew she wouldn't, so there wasn't much point in that. *Maybe if I keep her talking, she won't think about kissing me,* he thought, with sudden hope.

So he named some of his favorite books.

To his surprise, Mary Lou had read most of them. They got to arguing about who was better, C. S. Lewis or Natalie Babbitt, and before he knew it, they were standing at the corner near his house.

"Well, I gotta go," he said abruptly, when he realized where they were.

Mary Lou looked unhappy.

Jeremy might actually have considered continuing the conversation, except his stomach began to roar with hunger again.

"See you later!" he called, and ran for the house.

When he got to the front door, he paused long enough to look around. *I hope nobody saw me talking to Mary Lou!* he thought.

Before he could worry much about that embarrassing possibility, he was distracted by a terrible sound from his bedroom.

Bolting up the stairs, Jeremy threw open his door.

"Hey!" he cried angrily. "Stop that!"

The dragon, perched atop one of the gerbil cages, was hissing, shrieking, and flapping its tiny wings as if it wanted to lift the whole thing into the air. One terrified gerbil clung to the exercise wheel, shaking with fear. The other cowered in a corner, trying to hide under the sawdust.

"Stop that!" repeated Jeremy, running toward the cage. "Stop it right now!"

The dragon ignored him.

Jeremy dropped his books and reached out to

pull the dragon away from the cage. But between the creature's rapidly flapping wings and wide-open mouth, he couldn't figure out how to grab it. He kept reaching forward, then drawing his hands back. The dragon continued to strain at the cage.

Finally Jeremy closed his eyes and thought, as hard as he could: *STOP!*

To his surprise, it worked.

Somehow he knew, even though his eyes were still closed, that the dragon had turned toward him. Then it *sent* him a question.

The question didn't come in the form of a word, of course. It came in that now familiar sense of question-ness. Behind it were more questions, expressed half in feelings, half in fleeting images. He *saw* a picture of the dragon munching on a gerbil. With it came the sense that surely these rodents had no purpose other than to provide a dragon's dinner.

The other thing that accompanied the images was a ravening hunger. Suddenly Jeremy understood that it hadn't been his own appetite that had roused him from his reading at the library; it had been the dragon's, which he was somehow sharing. The sensation returned so powerfully that he began wishing he could munch on a gerbil himself.

"Blechh!" he said, opening his eyes. But his anger with the dragon dimmed when he remembered the porkchops he'd eaten for supper the night before.

"When you get right down to it, I suppose there's

not much difference between eating a pig and eating a guinea pig," he said, holding out his hand to the dragon. "And it's silly to be angry with you just for being hungry. 'No sense in getting mad at a cat for being a cat,' as Dad would say. But I'm going to have to get you to understand that pets aren't snacks."

The dragon was calmer now. It began crawling slowly up his arm. The feeling of the little claws against his skin made Jeremy twitch. About the time the dragon reached his elbow, Mrs. Thatcher stepped into the room.

"What is going on in here?" she demanded.

Terrified, Jeremy turned toward the door. He started to speak, then stopped. How could he possibly explain the dragon?

"What was all that noise?" continued Mrs. Thatcher. "I could hear it all the way out in the yard."

Jeremy blinked. Didn't she see the dragon? He flinched as one of its wingtips tickled his neck.

"What are you twitching about?" asked Mrs. Thatcher.

"Nothing!" said Jeremy, feeling somewhat dazed.

Mrs. Thatcher wrinkled her brow. "Well, what was all that noise up here a minute ago?"

"Some of the animals were fighting," said Jeremy, pulling his head sideways as the dragon nipped affectionately at his ear. (At least, he *hoped* the gesture was affectionate; it was hard to tell with a beast *that* hungry.)

"I never heard any of them make a sound like that before. Maybe you'd better split them up."

"I was just trying to figure out how to keep them apart when you came in," said Jeremy truthfully.

As he spoke, the dragon started to crawl from one of his shoulders to the other. He tried not to laugh as the wings tickled his neck.

"Well, let me know if you need another cage," said Mrs. Thatcher. "I think your dad has a few extras around his office. And stop wiggling, Jeremy. You look like you've got Saint Vitus' Dance!"

She started to leave, then turned back. "When you get things taken care of up here, I want you outside. Dad's got a full load of patients, and there's no reason I should have to do all the yard work myself."

"Sure," said Jeremy, still trying to figure out why his mother wasn't saying anything about the dragon. Was it possible that she couldn't see it? The idea was strange—but no stranger than the dragon itself.

His confusion was multiplied by the continuous waves of hunger coming from the dragon. He was having trouble concentrating, until he heard his mother's next sentence.

"By the way, your father's cooking up some business deal with the parents of one of the kids in your class. We're having the whole family over for dinner next week."

"Who?" asked Jeremy, hoping it wasn't Howard or Freddy.

"Their name is Hutton."

Jeremy screamed and flung himself across the bed, causing the dragon to flutter into the air. "My life is over," moaned Jeremy. "How could you do this to me?"

The dragon landed on the pillow. It stared at Jeremy, broadcasting crankiness about the sudden movement.

Mrs. Thatcher seemed to feel the same way. "What on earth is the matter with you?" she demanded.

"Are you really going to invite Mary Lou Hutton into this house?"

"Any reason why we shouldn't?"

"She's in love with me!"

Mrs. Thatcher smiled. "Well, I wouldn't take it too seriously, dear."

"You don't understand, Mom. She wants to kiss me!"

"Oh, well, I wouldn't let her do that. You're a little young to start that kind of thing."

"I don't *want* to let her do that! I want to stay as far away from her as I can!"

Mrs. Thatcher frowned. "I'm sure she'll behave herself during dinner, Jeremy. This is fairly important to your father, so I want you to be polite when they come."

Jeremy sighed. He could tell there was no point in trying to explain the total humiliation he would suffer if Howard Morton and Freddy the Frog Killer found out that Mary Lou had been to his house for dinner. It would be bad enough if they found out she had walked him home, which they probably would since she would probably tell everyone in school. Even Spess would have something to say about *that.* And it would give Howard, Freddy, and the others ammunition to make his life miserable for weeks.

"Anyway, I want you outside soon," said his mother. "And for goodness sake, stop *twitching!* You look like you're having a nervous breakdown."

He *felt* like he was having a nervous breakdown. He wanted to tell his mother that he would hold still if only the dragon would do the same. But there was no point in that, since then she would be sure he was crazy. So he just nodded and said, "I'll be down as soon as I can."

Well aware of Jeremy's sense of time, Mrs. Thatcher snorted and left the room.

As soon as she was gone, Jeremy plucked the dragon from his shoulder. "What is going on here?" he asked, looking straight into its emerald eyes.

SIX

Tiamat

The dragon squirmed, sending a message that felt like, "Let me go!"

Jeremy hesitated, then released his hold on the creature. Flapping its leathery wings, it flew to the top of his bookcase. The moment it landed, Jeremy was struck with another wave of hunger. Clearly, he wasn't going to get any answers until the beast was fed.

He listened for the sound of the back door. As soon as he was sure his mother was safely out in the yard, he darted down the stairs for more chicken livers. He took the dragon with him—just to be sure nothing happened while he was out of the room.

When the dragon had finally sated its hunger, it sat on Jeremy's desk, preening its scales with its beaky nose.

Jeremy stared at it. "All right," he said. "Give. Why didn't Mom say anything about you?"

No answer.

Jeremy tried again. Closing his eyes, he formed a mental image of his mother standing in the doorway. Then he tried to attach a sense of questionness to the picture.

The dragon responded by sending him a pair of pictures. The first showed Jeremy standing in front of his mother, with the dragon perched on his shoulder. Then the dragon faded from the image, until all Jeremy could see was himself. Standing there without the dragon he looked—as his mother had said—ridiculously twitchy.

The pictures triggered a memory of something Jeremy had read. *Do you mean Mom couldn't see you?* he thought. *Are you invisible to her?*

The dragon puffed a little cloud of smoke and sent Jeremy a confused jumble of colors.

Jeremy frowned. If he wanted to communicate with the dragon, he was going to have to learn to think in pictures. Probably not a bad habit for someone who wanted to be an artist. But it was going to take lot of practice before they could "talk" easily. Of course, the dragon was just a baby. In fact, given how young it was, the fact that they could communicate at all was pretty amazing. Jeremy wondered just how smart the beast was going to get.

"Well, if you stay invisible, it's going to be a lot easier to keep you a secret," he said. "As long as you don't do anything else to attract my parents' attention."

He glanced at the clock on his dresser. The lawn!

How long could he stall before his mother got upset?

It wasn't that he didn't *want* to help, though he certainly had better things to do with his time than work on the lawn—like drawing, for instance. But if he didn't get things under control here, who knew what kind of disaster he would find when he came back?

Setting his alarm to ring in ten minutes, Jeremy picked up the book Miss Priest had given him—the one written by S. H. Elives.

He had skimmed twenty pages before it occurred to him to see if the book had an index. It did. Feeling silly, he began flipping through the back pages. He decided to start with "taming." The index had the word, but rather than listing a page to turn to, it said in dark letters: **Don't even think of such a thing!**

A sudden squawk from the dragon distracted him. Turning, he saw that it had gotten into a fierce wrestling match with a dirty sock. As Jeremy watched, dragon and sock rolled across the floor and disappeared under his bed.

Jeremy decided to start at the top of the index and skim straight through. When he got to the word "milk" he remembered something he had read at the library. Flipping eagerly to the proper page, he found the following:

Though dragons are best known for rampaging through the countryside, eating sheep and

> shepherd alike, many of them are reputed to have a deep fondness for milk. In at least two instances, we are told of a village or castle that kept one of the great worms at bay by offering it a trough of milk every day. The dragon would drink the milk. Then, hunger sated, it would return to its cave for a long nap. This method was particularly effective in the case of the dragon of Lambton Hall.
>
> Whence this fondness for milk? No one is quite certain. Some think it may stem from the fact that dragon mothers cannot nurse their young, which leaves the little beasts with a lifelong craving for milk. Others think it has to do with the primal fluid of the universe. Many simply list it as one of the mysteries of dragondom. In any event, while the method is hardly foolproof, it is certainly worth trying if you should ever be faced with a marauding dragon.

"Or dragonlet," added Jeremy, as he closed the book. He felt a little foolish. He had read the story of the dragon of Lambton Hall at the library. Why hadn't it occurred to *him* to try the milk trick?

He glanced at the clock beside his bed. If he didn't get outside soon his mother would start to get cranky. Dashing down the stairs, he slipped into the kitchen and filled a saucer with milk. He looked at it, decided it might not be enough, and got out a soup bowl. After a second, he decided to take the entire carton of milk back to his room, too.

Setting the soup bowl on the floor beside his bed, Jeremy poured in some milk.

Within seconds the dragon crawled out from under the bed, its flickery red tongue darting ahead of it. When it found the milk it plunged its head into the bowl and began slurping. Soon it had finished the entire bowl—a huge amount for such a tiny dragon.

Jeremy poured some more milk into the bowl, but the dragon turned away and flapped its wings. Its stomach was so full that for all its efforts, it could get no more than a few inches off the floor.

Making a little growling noise, the dragon gave up the effort at flight, sank its claws into the sheets, and began to climb the bed. When it reached the top it curled up on Jeremy's pillow and fell fast asleep.

Jeremy smiled. If the book was right, the milk should hold it for the rest of the day.

If it wasn't, he didn't know what he was going to do.

When Jeremy returned from helping his mother, the dragon was no longer on the pillow. The only mark of its presence was a small brown spot where its breath had scorched the pillowcase.

"Dragon?" he said softly. "Dragon, where are you?"

A little swirl of blue trickled into his brain.

"Where are you?" asked Jeremy again.

The colors moved in a slow circle. It took Jeremy a moment to realize that the dragon was sleeping.

But where?

Jeremy finally found the beast curled up in his sock drawer. Even though he knew babies needed to sleep, he couldn't help himself. Reaching down, he scooped the dragon into his hands. It snorted and opened one eye. The expression on its face was cranky, and Jeremy's head began to swirl with irritated shades of brown and green.

But the dragon's mood passed quickly. Soon it had settled into the place on Jeremy's shoulder it seemed to have chosen as its special spot.

"Let's see if we can name you," said Jeremy. Plucking the dragon from his shoulder, he carried it to his desk. "Stay there for a minute," he said firmly.

The dragon's long tongue flicked out and back.

Jeremy found the list of great dragons that he had made at the library. "How about Fafnir?" he asked.

The dragon yawned.

Jeremy crossed the name off the list. "Smaug?"

The dragon curled its lip. Jeremy was just as glad; Smaug was the dragon in *The Hobbit,* and it had been a particularly wretched beast.

"Ouroboros?"

The dragon snorted, sending out a tiny puff of smoke. Jeremy wasn't sure if it was reacting to the name, or his attempt to pronounce it. He crossed it off anyway.

The dragon was no happier with Orm Emfax, Heart's Blood, Nmenth, or Ruth. It wasn't until Jeremy suggested "Tiamat" that a flood of approving color came swirling through his head.

"Tiamat?" he asked again.

The dragon squirmed with pleasure. Its tail tied itself in a knot.

Jeremy smiled. "Tiamat it is," he said. He was pleased. He never felt really at ease with a new pet until he had named it.

Jeremy hesitated. Maybe "it" was the wrong word. After all, according to Babylonian mythology, the original Tiamat was the mother dragon who had created the world. So Tiamat must be a female name. Did that mean his dragon was female, too?

Though the answer didn't really come as a word, there was no doubt it was a positive response.

Jeremy smiled. One mystery solved. He had a girl dragon, and her name was Tiamat.

He looked at the dragon nervously. Had he really named her—or had he just found the name she had wanted all along?

That thought opened his mind to a whole list of questions he had been trying to ignore, such as: Where had this thing really come from? What had Mr. Elives meant when he said, "*It* wants you"? And, most important, what was he supposed to do now?

He closed his eyes and tried to send these questions to the dragon. Aside from some general puzzlement, he got no response.

"Well, what did I expect?" he said aloud. "You're still a baby. Practically brand-new."

He stroked Tiamat's tiny head and wondered once again how big she was going to get. Though he hadn't really meant it as a question, she answered him anyway. And the image that formed in his mind left no doubt what the answer was.

BIG!

Jeremy swallowed hard. But before he could think anything back at her, a voice yelled, "Hey, Jer, are you up there?"

"Sure!" he yelled back. "Come on up, Spess."

He turned to the dragon, which was chewing on the end of one of his paintbrushes, and asked, "Now, will he be able to see you, or not?"

Tiamat flew up to his shoulder without answering.

"Where did you go yesterday?" asked Specimen, bursting into the room. "I looked all over for you. I've never seen anyone run so fast!"

"Do you blame me?" asked Jeremy, turning so that the dragon would be in clear view. He waited for Spess to say something about Tiamat.

But Specimen only shrugged and shook his head. "I'm just glad it was you and not me," he said.

"Thanks," replied Jeremy, a trifle bitterly.

Spess missed his tone. He looked troubled. "My sister Mindy said she saw you walking with Mary Lou this morning," he said at last.

Jeremy groaned. "Your sister's mouth is bigger than Alaska."

"Well," insisted Spess. "Were you?"

"No—she was walking with me. I had my arms full and couldn't run away."

Spess nodded as if that answer satisfied him. Then, as if a new thought had just struck him, he added, "Full of what?"

"Full of books. About—" Jeremy decided to be daring. "About dragons."

"You always did like that kind of stuff," said Specimen. His tone made it sound like he thought there was something slightly strange about that fact. "Want to work on our entries for the art contest?" he asked, changing the subject.

"I have to go out and finish raking," said Jeremy with a sigh.

The dragon crawled down his arm and onto the desk. She stared at Specimen as if memorizing his features. The question she sent Jeremy seemed to translate as "Friend or foe?"

Friend, thought Jeremy. *Old friend.*

Specimen proved it by helping Jeremy rake. When they were done, Jeremy went upstairs to check on the dragon, who was once more snoozing among his socks. He moved one pair that was too close to her nose, hoping his mother wouldn't notice the little scorch marks.

"Come with me," he said to Spess, who had

watched in mystification while Jeremy peered into his sock drawer, "I want you to help me find something."

"What?"

"A magic shop."

SEVEN

Still Life

Jeremy and Spess wandered around for nearly two hours without finding a trace of Mr. Elives' shop. It seemed to have vanished from the face of the earth.

"Come on, Jeremy," said Spess at last. "I'm getting tired."

Back at his house, Jeremy tried the phone book. But he found no listing for "Elives' Magic Supplies," not even in the yellow pages. When he dialed information, the operator said, "I'm sorry, sir, but there is no such business."

"What's so important about this place, anyway?" asked Specimen.

Jeremy couldn't figure out a way to explain without telling Spess things he shouldn't. Because they were both tired, this led to an argument.

"Fine!" shouted Specimen. "Next time take Mary Lou with you!" Grabbing a pile of art supplies he had loaned Jeremy the week before, he stormed out of the room.

Great, thought Jeremy glumly. *Now even my best friend is mad at me.*

Tiamat poked her head over the edge of the sock drawer. A comfortable swirl of yellow flowed into Jeremy's mind.

But then, maybe I've got a new best friend, he thought with a smile.

He decided to read some of the book Miss Priest had given him. Unfortunately, it seemed to have vanished in the general chaos of his room.

"Just my luck," he groaned, throwing himself on his bed.

"I don't want to go to school," he said, when his mother set a fried egg in front of him on Monday morning. Poking a hole in the yolk, he watched the yellow goo ooze across his plate.

"Can't say as I blame you," said his father. "School is a repressive institution, aimed at subduing the masses. Still and all, it's easier to send you than to have you underfoot. So off you go."

"Herb!" cried Mrs. Thatcher. "That's a terrible thing to say."

"It's a sad thing but trooo-o-o," warbled Jeremy's father, reaching for the blueberry granola. He began pouring the cereal into his "Roy'n'Trigger" bowl and added, "But then, life's tough. Isn't it, Jer?"

Jeremy nodded glumly, and tried not to squirm when his mother put her hand on his forehead.

"You haven't got a fever," she said, sounding relieved. "My diagnosis is Monday-morning-osis. I'm afraid your dad is right. About going, that is," she added, giving Dr. Thatcher a sharp look.

Jeremy finished his egg and trudged out of the room. He didn't care about repressive institutions and he certainly didn't plan to be underfoot. But he did have three very good reasons for wanting to stay home. The first was to remain with Tiamat. The second was to avoid Howard, Freddy, and Mary Lou. The third was to turn his room inside out looking for Miss Priest's book.

At least the milk trick is working, he thought, as he went out the door. *With that bowl of milk inside her, Tiamat should doze all day.*

Actually, his main concern now was the rate at which she was growing. Her head, which had been no bigger than his thumb when she hatched, was already the size of a lemon.

He wandered along the sidewalk, wondering what new horrors the day might hold. For one bright moment he thought that if last Friday's humiliating scene with Mr. Kravitz had been the worst moment of his life, maybe from here on in things would get better.

Somehow, he doubted it.

"Hey, Jeremy!" cried Spess, as Jeremy, still wrapped in gloom, trudged along the sidewalk in front of the Bothill home. "Wait up!"

Jeremy smiled as Spess came bumbling down the front steps of his house. At least his friend was talking to him again. But before they really started to feel comfortable with each other, they heard a shrill whistle. Turning, they saw Martha Colgin standing at the corner. Taking a silver coach's whistle from her lips, she screamed, "Mary Lou, I found Jeremy. He's over this way."

"Uh-oh," said Specimen. "Looks like you'd better—"

But Jeremy was already gone. Sprinting for all he was worth, he ran the entire distance to school. He knew he would be safe once he reached his homeroom. Their teacher, Mr. Sigel, didn't put up with that kind of nonsense.

Unfortunately, there were times in the school day when Mr. Sigel wasn't around. Howard Morton, who had seen Jeremy's mad dash from Mary Lou, started making loud, wet, kissing noises every time Jeremy walked past him on the playground.

Even worse, Mary Lou told some of her friends that she was going to Jeremy's house for dinner that weekend, with the result that by the time Friday rolled around, people were chanting "Jeremy Thatcher and Hot Stuff Hutton—the Ro-o-o-omance of the Century!" every time they saw him.

Jeremy was so tired of the whole thing that he began to wish Tiamat was big enough to start eating some of the people who were really bugging him.

At least Spess hadn't gone over to the enemy camp. When Howard made his kissing sound at Jeremy as they were walking into art on Friday afternoon, Spess whispered, "Maybe you should just punch him out."

"What a great idea!" replied Jeremy. "Heck, he's only a foot and a half taller than me."

Specimen looked hurt. "Well, at least he would know you were serious."

"Specimen, the day Howard takes me seriously, I'm in *real* trouble."

They had to stop talking then, because Mr. Kravitz had lumbered to the front of the room. "Today we are going to draw still lifes," said the teacher. He directed their attention to a small round table that held two oranges, a banana, and a tall blue water jug.

After Mr. Kravitz had spent some time telling them what a wonderful job he had done in arranging the items, he passed out paper and said, "Start drawing."

Jeremy began to sketch, slowly at first, then with growing enthusiasm. Soon he was so involved with what he was doing that he didn't notice Mr. Kravitz standing behind him. He jumped when the gruff voice said, "Perhaps you did not understand me, Mr. Thatcher. We are drawing still lifes today. In particular, *that* still life."

He gestured to the table in the middle of the room, then to Jeremy's picture. The banana and the oranges looked fine. But instead of the blue jug, Jeremy had drawn a small dragon trying to eat one of the oranges, which was bigger than its head.

"*That* is not a still life," said Mr. Kravitz, his voice dripping with sarcasm. "In fact, it is not based on any kind of life at all. I did not ask you to use your imagination today. I asked you to use your eyes—to draw what you see."

Jeremy wanted to say, "This *is* what I see. It's what's inside me." But before he could find the courage to speak, Mr. Kravitz slapped his hand against the desk.

"I want fruit," he roared. "Fruit, Thatcher, not imaginary animals!"

"But it's NOT . . ."

Jeremy stopped himself. What was he going to do? Tell Mr. Kravitz the dragon was real? Even if he did tell about Tiamat, no one else could see her.

"Try again, Thatcher," said Mr. Kravitz, handing Jeremy a fresh sheet of paper.

Jeremy sighed. When he wanted more paper, he couldn't get it. When he was happy with what he was doing, Mr. Kravitz took it away and told him to start over.

He considered adding Mr. Kravitz to the next drawing. After all, the man *was* shaped like a pear. He decided the joke would be more trouble than it was worth.

Reluctantly, he picked up his pencil and started to sketch. He was blocking in the banana when a jolt of pain surged through his head. He cried out in shock, his hand jerking out of control and knocking a box of charcoal sticks across the table.

"Hey!" cried Specimen, as the brittle sticks of

charcoal went cascading over his drawing. "Watch it!"

Jeremy barely heard him. Something was wrong with Tiamat. Glancing up, he saw Mr. Kravitz heading in their direction. He looked angrier than ever.

No time to worry about that. "Gonna throw up!" he yelled, jumping to his feet and heading for the door. That would slow Mr. Kravitz down. Everyone knew he hated it when kids puked.

Dashing into the hall, Jeremy raced for the back door of the school and started across the playground. Realizing he was more apt to be spotted that way, he changed direction, taking the longer route down Cherry Street toward the park. By the time he reached the park entrance, his lungs felt like there were little men inside scrubbing them with sandpaper.

But he kept running.

Gasping for breath, he stumbled up the front steps of his house, fumbled with the key, threw open the door, and shot into the living room.

To his surprise, everything was quiet. He had expected chaos, an ongoing uproar. But the house was silent. Even the bounding enthusiasm of Grief was missing.

Stopping to catch his breath, Jeremy suddenly realized that the sense of panic and danger filling his head had faded. He had been so wound up in trying to get home, he had not noticed the ebbing of the crisis until now. The searing pain created by his desperate sprint had blocked any sendings he might have received from Tiamat.

He started up the stairs, but a soft whine stopped him. Turning, he saw that it came from Grief, who was cowering under the dining room table.

What's been going on here? he wondered. *Where's Tiamat?*

The instant he thought the question, he sensed the dragon's location. It wasn't anything as simple as a message saying, "I'm here." He just knew where she was.

Bounding up the stairs, he stopped at his door, appalled by the mess that greeted him. His room, never very neat at its best, looked like a hurricane had just passed through. The general clutter that usually hid the floor appeared to have been whipped around with a giant eggbeater. The covers had been pulled off his bed. Anything that could be tipped over, had been.

An indignant squawk drew his attention to Tiamat. She was perched on top of the bookshelf, glaring down at him angrily. However, the feeling he was picking up from her was not anger with him but at the world in general.

"What is it?" he asked gently, picking his way across the debris-covered floor. "What's wrong, Ti?"

Tiamat opened her mouth and hissed. Jeremy drew back for a second, then stepped forward again. The dragonlet looked different than she had that morning—lighter, somehow, as if someone had polished her scales. Suddenly he spotted something that looked like a piece of red cellophane lying on the bookshelf.

"Your skin!" he said breathlessly. "Ti—you've shed your skin."

Holding out his hand, he invited Tiamat to climb onto his shoulder. She was partway up his arm when Jeremy heard a noise that startled him. He spun around so fast that Tiamat had to grab his sleeve with her teeth to keep from falling off. She sent him a flash of angry purple to let him know she didn't appreciate that kind of sudden movement.

Jeremy ignored the sending. He was too upset by what he saw.

EIGHT

The Dragon Who Came to Dinner

Mary Lou Hutton stood in Jeremy's doorway, staring at him with wide blue eyes. Though her lips were moving, nothing came out.

"What are *you* doing here?" he demanded furiously.

Mary Lou found her voice at last. "You've got a dragon!"

"That's none of your business! Why are you—" Then it hit him. "You mean you can see her?"

Before Mary Lou could answer, Jeremy was distracted by Tiamat launching herself into the air. He winced as a sharp pain shot through his shoulder. At first, he thought the dragon's claws had caused it. But when he pulled back the neck of his T-shirt he saw that the skin underneath was unmarked. He cried out as another jab of pain shot along his arm. What was going on here?

Turning to Tiamat, he noticed that the dragonlet was favoring her right wing—flying with a limp, so to speak. Being linked into her head, he was sharing her pain. He rubbed his shoulder in relief when Tiamat settled on top of the door to stare down at Mary Lou.

"It's beautiful," said Mary Lou. "Only, it's kind of scary."

"It's not an it," said Jeremy. "It's a she. And how come you can see her?"

Mary Lou looked puzzled, and Jeremy realized it had been a stupid question. How would Mary Lou know why she could see the dragon, when she didn't even know that she shouldn't be able to? But stupid question or not, he needed an answer. Of all the people in the world Tiamat might have revealed herself to, why did she choose Mary Lou Hutton?

"I love dragons," said Mary Lou, as if she were answering him.

Jeremy stared at her in surprise. Had she just read his mind? Since she was still gazing at Tiamat, Jeremy decided Mary Lou's comment had been nothing more than talk. Then he wondered if Mary Lou had accidentally answered his question anyway. Did loving dragons have something to do with being able to see them? Or had Tiamat just been so distracted by shedding her skin that she had forgotten to make herself invisible?

"You're the first person besides me who's been able to see her," said Jeremy.

Mary Lou took far more pleasure in this fact than did Jeremy. "Wow," she said, her face glowing. "That's neat. Where did you get her, anyway?"

"I don't think I'm supposed to tell. Besides, it's none of your business. And you still haven't told me what you're doing here."

"I came to see if you were all right."

Jeremy stared at her, waiting for her to explain.

"Well, when I was coming back from the girl's room I saw you go rushing out of the school. You had such a terrible look on your face, I decided to follow you. When I got here, the front door was wide open. I thought maybe something horrible had happened, so I came in." She paused. "Are you okay?"

Jeremy wanted to tell Mary Lou to stop asking questions and scram. But the fact that she had seen Tiamat made him feel—oddly—that she had some kind of right to be here.

"Are you okay?" she repeated.

"I'm not sure. Something was wrong with Tiamat."

An image flashed into his mind. Jeremy closed his eyes. In his head, he saw Tiamat rolling her shoulders as she tried to shed her skin.

"Jeremy!" cried Mary Lou. "What are you doing?"

Jeremy opened his eyes. He had been rotating his shoulders as if he were trying to shed his own skin. He blushed. This nonverbal communication of Tiamat's was starting to get out of hand!

"Tiamat was shedding," he explained. "It frightened her."

Another image came into his head. "But that wasn't all. While she was trying to get out of her skin, my dog, Grief, came through the door to investigate."

"Did he hurt her?" asked Mary Lou breathlessly.

Jeremy shook his head. "I doubt it. He's trained to leave the animals alone. But I bet he tried to pick her up. After all, he's a retriever, and—"

Jeremy broke off as Tiamat began sending him images of the wild scramble that had followed Grief's entry into the room. He was appalled by the dragon's ferocity. No wonder Grief was hiding under the table!

He shook his head to clear it. "The whole thing was my fault," he said, blushing a little. "I try to keep the door closed, but I guess I had so much on my mind this morning that I didn't pull it tight. Thank goodness I gave Tiamat her milk before I went to school. No telling what she might have done to Grief if she hadn't been feeling sluggish."

"Milk?"

"It keeps her calm," said Jeremy. He paused, then added, "Listen, Mary Lou. You have to promise not to tell anyone about this."

Mary Lou looked offended. "Of course I won't tell anyone. I know how these things work!"

Jeremy remembered their conversation about books the day Mary Lou had followed him home from the library. Maybe if someone had to find out about Tiamat, it was just as well that it was someone like her.

But Jeremy's good feelings about Mary Lou vanished when she asked, "What are we going to do now?"

"*We* aren't going to do anything," he snapped. "This is *my* problem. What *you're* going to do is go away."

"I just wanted to help," said Mary Lou, her lip trembling.

"I don't need your help!" said Jeremy. "No one invited you to come barging in here!"

"Well, excuse me for caring!" yelled Mary Lou. Turning, she ran out of the room.

Jeremy listened as she raced down the stairs and out the front door.

"Oh, shut up," he said, when Tiamat sent her question feeling. He was confused. Tiamat was all right. Mary Lou was gone. He should be happy.

So why do I feel so lousy? he wondered.

He decided to work on his room. Tolerant as his mother was of his usual mess level, there was no way she was going to let him get away with this.

Maybe I'll at least find Miss Priest's book, he thought, as he pulled the sheet back onto the bed.

But after nearly three hours of work he hadn't found the slightest trace of the book. He was upset, both because he really wanted to read it—and because he was worried about what Miss Priest was going to do if he couldn't find it. He had a feeling it was very valuable.

As if things weren't bad enough already, that night at supper his mother reminded him that the Huttons were coming to dinner on Sunday.

The only good thing about the whole day was the beautiful colors Tiamat sent into his head as he was going to sleep.

"What's the big deal, anyway?" asked Jeremy on Sunday afternoon as he watched his mother prepare for the dinner party. "You'd think the president was coming or something."

"Don't be silly," said Mrs. Thatcher. She flipped the pie dough she was working on and pressed it lightly with her rolling pin. "I just want to make a nice meal."

"And I want *you* to be on your best behavior, Buster," said his father, who happened to wander into the kitchen at that moment. "I don't want you chasing our guests' little girl around and trying to kiss her."

"Dad!" cried Jeremy, totally disgusted.

"Go cut some rhubarb, Herb," said Mrs. Thatcher.

"I'm busy," said Dr. Thatcher.

"Doing what?"

"Bothering Jeremy."

"Herbert Thatcher, you go cut that rhubarb, or you can cook this meal yourself."

Dr. Thatcher shrugged. "See that, kid," he said.

"She's on your side." He winked at Jeremy, then sauntered out the back door, singing some old song about rhubarb. He tripped over a cat as he went.

By six o'clock the house was filled with delicious aromas. Jeremy felt his mouth begin to water as he sat in his room, trying to communicate with Tiamat. He loved it when she sent swirls of color into his head, but he wanted to learn to speak to her more clearly.

"Jeremy!" called his mother. "The Huttons are here!"

"Great," he grumbled. He dragged down the stairs, trying to convince himself it was possible to be nice to Mary Lou.

While the adults greeted each other enthusiastically, Mary Lou and Jeremy glared at each other.

"Jeremy, why don't you show Mary Lou around the office," said Dr. Thatcher. "I understand she's a real animal lover."

When Jeremy rolled his eyes, his father shot him a look that said very clearly, "Be nice, or you're dead meat."

He decided to show Mary Lou the office. "This way," he said, making sure to keep far enough away that she couldn't sneak in a kiss when he wasn't looking.

"I'm sorry I barged into your room on Friday," said Mary Lou, as they walked down the path behind the house.

Jeremy shrugged. "Forget it," he said, opening the office door.

"I didn't tell anyone about the dragon," said Mary Lou, once they were inside.

Jeremy laughed. "Do you think they would have believed you if you had?"

"Probably not. Good grief. That's the biggest cat I've ever seen!"

Mary Lou was standing in front of Fat Pete, who had come in for more stitches that morning.

"Probably the crankiest, too," said Jeremy, as Mary Lou reached her hand toward the cage. "I wouldn't . . ."

His words were too late. Pete swatted at Mary Lou.

"Ouch!" she cried, pulling her hand back. "You rotten thing!"

"No sense in getting mad at a cat for being a cat," said Jeremy. "Come on. We've got stuff to put on that."

While Jeremy doctored Mary Lou's hand they started to talk about books. By the time they returned to the house they were deep in an argument about the *Chronicles of Narnia.* Jeremy ran up to his room to get *Prince Caspian* to prove a point to Mary Lou.

He found one of Tiamat's teeth beside the bookshelf, and deposited it in the collection he had started in his desk.

When he left the room he closed the door carefully, to avoid a repeat of the disaster with Grief. Unfortunately, while he was concentrating on shutting the dog *out,* he forgot to worry about keeping the dragon *in.* Though Jeremy didn't know it, Tiamat was already in the hall when the door clicked shut.

Jeremy rejoined Mary Lou in the living room. But before he could find the page he was looking for, his mother called them to supper.

They were eating in the dining room, which proved it was a special occasion—as did the fact that his mother had bought new candles. Jeremy felt a great longing in his head when she lit them. He blinked. The feeling came from Tiamat.

Fire! she thought happily, flying into the room.

Jeremy dropped his fork. Mary Lou gasped.

"What's wrong with you two?" asked Dr. Thatcher.

"Nothing!" they said in unison.

"Kids," said Mary Lou's father, as if that explained everything.

Fire! sang Tiamat in Jeremy's head. She landed on his shoulder and began to crawl down to the table.

NO! thought Jeremy desperately. *Not now! Go away!*

Tiamat glared at him angrily. Then she turned and flew from the room. Mrs. Hutton blinked, looking puzzled by the sudden breeze created by Tiamat's wings.

Once the dragon was gone, Jeremy felt better—until he heard the yowl from the kitchen.

"What in heaven's name was that?" said Dr. Thatcher.

He started to his feet, but before he could get

away from the table, one of the kitchen cats came streaking into the dining room.

"Oh!" cried Mary Lou's mother. "Get it away from me. I can't stand cats!"

That was unfortunate, since at that moment three more cats came running into the room. Tiamat was flying after them, snapping at their tails. The first cat dashed under the table. So did two of the next three.

The fourth, however, which was the one Tiamat was closest to catching, jumped right onto the table.

The adults all began to yell at once. With that much noise, Jeremy didn't figure anyone would hear him, so he shouted, "Tiamat, cut that out!"

The dragon ignored him. The cat was careening around the table, stepping on people's plates and knocking over glasses.

One of the under-table cats began climbing onto Mrs. Hutton's lap.

"Get it away!" she screamed. As she jumped to her feet, the cat sprang forward onto the table.

Now there were two cats scrambling among the dishes, with Tiamat chasing after both of them.

"Herbert!" cried Mrs. Thatcher. *"Do something!"*

Dr. Thatcher dived for one of the cats, missed, and landed face first in the mashed potatoes. A cat ran over his head.

Mary Lou's father tried next. His hand came down on the edge of a plate, which sailed into the air, spraying gravy across the room.

The commotion attracted Grief, who ran into the room to see what all the excitement was about. He took one look at Tiamat and began barking and lunging at her. His front paws landed on the table. He tried to scramble up to join the chase, but only succeeded in pulling the tablecloth down onto himself.

With a resounding crash, everything—plates, candles, silverware, and food—fell to the floor. Grief ran howling from the room.

Jeremy looked at the clock. Dinner had started at 6:30. It had taken only until 6:32 to turn the room into a total shambles.

NINE

The Heat Is On

Mrs. Hutton was a mess. Mr. Hutton was furious. Mrs. Thatcher was crying. And Dr. Thatcher, his face still dotted with mashed potatoes, was laughing so hard he could barely stand up.

"People always laugh about this kind of thing after they get done being upset," he told Jeremy later. "The Huttons will be telling this story for years. I figure, why wait? If I'm going to be amused later, I might as well be amused right now."

As none of the other adults seemed to share Dr. Thatcher's philosophy, the evening came to an early, uneasy end: "A premature death," as Dr. Thatcher phrased it.

Even though no one blamed Jeremy for the trouble, he spent the rest of the night wallowing in guilt.

Things didn't improve any the next morning when Mary Lou caught him on the way to school.

He had too many other things on his mind to

try to escape her, so she walked all the way to school with him. The fact that she didn't try to kiss him didn't stop Howard and Freddy from making loud, sloppy smacking sounds as soon as Jeremy and Mary Lou entered the building.

While Jeremy was trying to decide whether taking a pop at one of them was worth getting beat up for, the principal walked up and said, "I want to see the two of you in my office."

Jeremy's stomach began to squirm so violently that he felt as though he had swallowed something that was still alive. *What now?* he wondered miserably, as they followed Mr. Martinez.

"You first, Mr. Thatcher," said the principal. He gestured for Jeremy to take a seat inside, then sat behind his own desk. Folding his hands in front of him, he said, "Are you having trouble in art class?"

To Jeremy's surprise, the man's voice was mild, almost friendly. Even more surprising was the effect this question had on Jeremy's emotions. He felt as if Mr. Martinez had unlocked something hidden deep inside him. A flood of anger and sorrow raged through his body, and tears pricked at the corners of his eyes. He knew if he tried to talk, he would break down and sob.

The storm of emotion disturbed Tiamat. At the back of his head he could sense her stirring from her slumber.

Mr. Martinez stared at him. "I said, are you having trouble in art class?"

Still afraid to speak, Jeremy nodded.

Mr. Martinez looked away. "Not every teacher is right for every student," he said at last.

Jeremy was surprised by the gentleness in his voice.

Mr. Martinez straightened his tie. "If you have another day when you just can't cope with art, why don't you come down here for a little while?"

Jeremy tried to answer, but couldn't get the words past the lump in his throat.

"Do you understand me?" asked the principal. His voice had a harder edge now. "If you can't cope, you can come here. But don't just take off. I can't let you do that."

Jeremy nodded numbly. Mr. Martinez escorted him out of the office, then gestured to Mary Lou.

"Did he yell at you?" she whispered, as she walked past Jeremy. Her eyes were wide.

He shook his head. He started walking toward the classroom, then decided to wait for Mary Lou. When she came out, they walked back to the room together. "He didn't yell at me either," said Mary Lou, sounding relieved.

Specimen rolled his eyes when he saw the two of them enter. Jeremy wanted to explain, but he still didn't trust himself to say anything. A large chunk of emotion seemed to have lodged in his throat and he wasn't sure he could get any words past it without cutting the emotion loose, too. Since he wasn't interested in spending the next several minutes crying in front of the entire class, he remained silent.

During recess he didn't join the baseball game, as he normally would have. Instead, he sat under one of the small trees that had been planted when the school was built. He was scratching a picture in the dirt with a stick when he noticed a strange shadow in front of him.

Looking up, he saw Tiamat circling overhead. Her red wings looked like streamers of blood in the afternoon sunshine.

How did you get here? thought Jeremy in panic.

The dragon coasted down to his shoulder. She was nearly as long as his arm now, and he lurched a little with the weight of her.

He hadn't framed his question in a form she could understand, so he got no answer. He paused. Figuring out the best way to communicate with the dragon was like working a puzzle. Finally he sent a mental image of Tiamat sleeping at home, along with the question feeling.

Tiamat's response was a picture of himself, looking sad.

He took this to mean she had been worried about him. But how had she gotten out of his room—not to mention the house?

Her answer made him a little nervous about just how smart she was getting to be. It consisted of a series of pictures. In the first she flew up to the ceiling and began puffing at the smoke detector mounted above his door. The second showed Jeremy's father rushing into the room, looking worried. The third showed Tiamat taking advantage of the open door to escape from his room. Finally she offered him an image of the little door the cats used to go in and out—a door just wide enough for a small dragon, if it folded its wings tightly against its sides.

Go home! thought Jeremy, sending her an image of herself returning through the little door.

Tiamat's response felt like a frown inside his head. She didn't want to go home. He felt bad, and he needed her here.

I feel fine! insisted Jeremy. But it's hard to lie when you're communicating with thoughts instead of words. He didn't feel fine, and they both knew it. So Tiamat stayed.

As if things weren't bad enough, Mary Lou showed up next. "She's here!" she cried in delight.

Jeremy nodded.

"How come the others don't see her?"

Jeremy shrugged. "There's a lot about dragons I haven't figured out."

Tiamat sent him a little wave of smugness.

To his enormous relief, Mr. Sigel waved his hand to announce it was time to go back inside. They started toward the door, Jeremy hanging back a little so that no one would accidentally touch Tiamat.

Go home! he urged again as the line approached the school.

Tiamat refused. Jeremy trudged into the building, carrying the dragon on his shoulder.

In the classroom Tiamat slithered down Jeremy's arm, crawled under his desk, and curled up at his feet. She lay there, snoozing contentedly, while he worked on his math test.

He was glad she had consumed all her milk that morning. He was giving it to her in a mixing bowl now, and she was gulping down at least a quart at a time. Jeremy frowned. His parents were already wondering where all the milk was going. Before long he would have to start buying it out of his allowance.

I suppose it's worth it to keep her calm, he thought. He checked under his desk. She raised her head and gave him a dreamy dragon smile. He smiled back. They had made it through the first half hour without any trouble. And her presence actually had helped him calm down. That was partly out of necessity. If he didn't force himself to be calm, who knew what Tiamat might do?

He finished his test and looked around. Mary Lou was staring at him. When she saw him look at her she blushed and smiled.

What the heck? he thought, and smiled back.

Her blush deepened to crimson, and she turned away.

Jeremy was surprised. Maybe he wasn't powerless against Mary Lou after all. *I wonder what would happen if I sent a note saying I wanted to kiss her? Would she run away and leave me alone for good?*

He shook his head. What if she took him seriously? The risk definitely was not worth it.

As Mr. Sigel was collecting the tests, someone knocked at the door. Before anyone could get up, the door swung open. Mr. Kravitz stepped in.

Jeremy's reaction to the man woke Tiamat, who poked her head out from under the desk.

"I've come to discuss the Spring Art Contest," said Mr. Kravitz.

Jeremy's interest perked up. This was what he had been waiting for!

"As you know, the contest is sponsored by the Downtown Merchants' Association. They want things they can use to decorate their storefronts. As always, the grand winner gets to paint the giant window of Zambreno's Department Store.

"You're all invited to enter. *But*—I don't want to see anything but your best work. This contest is going to represent the school, and I want us to look good."

That made sense. But true to his fashion, Mr. Kravitz managed to say it in a way that made it seem very insulting. As the man talked, Jeremy found himself getting angrier and angrier. He knew it was a bad idea, but he couldn't help himself. It wasn't until he saw Tiamat slinking down the aisle that he realized what a major mistake it was to let his emotions get out of hand.

Tiamat! he thought desperately. *Get back here!*

Since he forgot to frame the command in pictures, the dragon ignored him. He searched for an image, then sent a picture of Tiamat crawling back under his desk.

She responded with a picture of Mr. Kravitz hopping around on one foot.

Jeremy's heart began to pound. *What are you up to?*

No answer.

Mr. Kravitz launched into a lecture on his standards for entries he was willing to submit to the merchants' association. "I don't want any of this green sky and pink grass stuff that some of you like to do," he said.

Jeremy heard Mary Lou gasp as Tiamat reached the front of the room and crouched beside Mr. Kravitz's left foot.

"After all," continued the art teacher, "I'm not going to have the people of this town think I haven't taught you anything about color."

Jeremy, watching Tiamat warily, doubted that anyone would believe a sixth grader who colored grass pink was doing anything but having fun.

"And I don't want any of this fantasy stuff," continued Mr. Kravitz, as Tiamat began to breathe on his foot. "No dragons, or any nonsense like that."

Yeah, let's not use our imaginations, thought Jeremy bitterly. By this time he was so fed up with Mr. Kravitz he didn't really care what Tiamat did. He watched her ribs rise and fall as she puffed on the art teacher's foot.

"And another thing," said Mr. Kravitz. He was starting to look uncomfortable now, and he lifted his foot to rub it against the back of his trousers. "I want you to—to—" Suddenly he bent down and stared at his shoe. Tiamat gave another puff, and it started to smoke.

Mr. Kravitz tore off the shoe and began hopping about on one foot. "Ooooowwww!" he cried. "Ow, ow, ow!"

It was just like the image Tiamat had sent to Jeremy. He could sense her smugness as she slithered back to his desk, and he had to bite down on the corners of his mouth to kill his laughter.

Mr. Sigel jumped up and stared at Mr. Kravitz. He started forward, then stopped, as if he couldn't figure out what to do.

Mr. Kravitz stared at his shoe in puzzlement. Most of the kids sat in wide-eyed astonishment. Given the art teacher's temper, Jeremy knew this was the safest reaction. Even so, from here and there around the room he could hear little snorts of laughter. Mary Lou, the only kid besides Jeremy who knew what had really happened, had her hands over her mouth.

Mr. Kravitz glared at the offenders. "I do not find this very amusing!" he shouted. He examined his shoe carefully, searching for signs of tampering. "I want to know who did this," he said. "And I want to know *now*."

When no one answered, Mr. Kravitz grew even angrier. "That does it!" he roared. "Until the coward who did this confesses, Room Nineteen is banned from the art contest."

Tucking his scorched shoe under his arm, he stormed out of the room, giving the door a wall-rattling slam as he left.

The class breathed out together, as if on some kind of signal.

"Can he really do that?" asked Specimen, his voice trembling.

"Do what?" asked Mr. Sigel.

"Ban us from the art contest."

Their teacher frowned. "Probably."

The look on Specimen's face twisted Jeremy's stomach.

Tiamat sent the question feeling, but Jeremy didn't know how to respond. The whole problem seemed too complicated to put into images. An hour ago he and Specimen had seemed like sure winners. Now in order for either of them to enter the contest, he, Jeremy, would have to confess to something he hadn't done—and confess it to the man he disliked most in the whole world.

TEN

✣

The Hatchers

"I can't believe it," said Specimen, as they trudged home that afternoon. "We've been waiting six years to win this contest!"

"I know," said Jeremy glumly.

He also knew that unless he was willing to face Mr. Kravitz, there was no chance for either of them to enter.

The idea was appalling. If he did confess, what was he going to say when Mr. Kravitz asked, as he was bound to, how Jeremy had done it? *Honesty might be the best policy,* thought Jeremy, *but it's kind of tough when the truth is something no one will believe.*

Tiamat wheeled overhead, sending occasional messages of concern. She stayed with them the same way a puppy would, first sprinting ahead, then falling back to investigate something, circling around them, eager to play.

Her antics made it hard to pay attention to Specimen.

Why can't Spess *see the dragon,* thought Jeremy miserably, *instead of Mary Lou?*

His thoughts were interrupted by a wave of gold washing through his head. Looking up, he saw Tiamat wheeling through the sky, looking like a string of rubies in the sunshine. Jeremy loved the sight. But it also troubled him. He had a feeling that dragons didn't really belong in this world anymore.

Or did they? If Tiamat was invisible to almost everyone else, was it possible there were other dragons, ones that *he* couldn't see? For a moment the idea that the world might be filled with invisible wonders filled his head. Who knew how many amazing things were out there, unknown, waiting to be discovered?

"Whatcha looking at?" asked Specimen.

"Just thinking," said Jeremy.

"You've been doing that a lot lately. Wanna come in and have something to eat?"

Before Jeremy could answer, Specimen smacked himself in the head and said, "I've got something that belongs to you!"

"What?"

"A book. I accidentally brought it home with some of my art stuff that day I got mad at you. It looks good, if you like that kind of stuff."

"What book?" asked Jeremy, hardly daring to hope.

Specimen shrugged. "Something about disappearing dragons."

Jeremy couldn't believe it. Miss Priest's book had been here all along! He didn't know whether to shout with relief—or clobber Specimen for causing him so much worry.

"I can't really stay," he said, which was more than true, considering the fact that he had a loose dragon to keep an eye on. "But I need that book."

Specimen looked hurt.

Jeremy continued home, clutching Miss Priest's book to his chest. He couldn't believe it had been in Specimen's room all this time. He couldn't wait to get home and read it!

A few blocks past Specimen's house he heard a yowl from the bushes beside him. He paused. The yowl came again. It sounded like a cat in pain.

Plunging through the leaves, Jeremy cried out in shock. There under the tree was Fat Pete. His legs had been tied together—front leg to front leg, back leg to back leg—and he was hopping about, trying to escape his tormentor, Freddy the Frog Killer, who was poking at him with a stick and laughing hysterically.

"You stop that!" cried Jeremy.

Freddy turned around. His cheeks were red, and Jeremy could tell he was angry at being caught in his nasty game. "Who's going to make me?" he snarled.

"Just stop it," said Jeremy, painfully aware that he was too small to *make* Freddy do anything.

To his amazement, Freddy did stop. "You're such a jerk, Thatcher," he sneered. Throwing down the stick, he brushed past Jeremy toward the sidewalk.

Jeremy held his breath until Freddy was past him. He was just about to breathe out when a ferocious kick caught him in the rear and sent him sprawling face first into the dirt.

"A jerk!" repeated Freddy. "Also, a . . . "

He didn't have time to finish explaining what Jeremy was, because Tiamat attacked. It would have worked better if Freddy had been able to see her. Then her claws, her jaws, her very strangeness might have frightened him into backing away. As it was, he only felt something unknown land on his chest and start to claw at him. Screaming, he flailed his arms in front of him. The frantic action knocked the little dragon into a bush.

Red swirls of pain streamed through Jeremy's brain.

"Tiamat!" he cried in horror.

Freddy's face was white. "You're weird, Thatcher!" he screamed, just before he turned and ran.

Jeremy groaned and pushed himself to his feet. Fat Pete howled, but Jeremy walked past him; except for his dignity, the bound cat was unharmed. Tiamat, however, was caught in the branches of a thorny bush, and her struggles to escape were only making the situation worse.

Stop! thought Jeremy. *Let me help you!*

Tiamat panted with exertion, her hot breath withering the leaves around her.

Stop, thought Jeremy again. *You're going to hurt yourself.*

She slowed her struggles. Working carefully, Jeremy extracted her from the bush. Though the thorns had scraped her wings, they were leathery and too tough to be easily pierced.

Nasty! she thought, sending pictures of both Freddy and the bush.

Jeremy couldn't have agreed more.

With Tiamat perched on his shoulder, he untied Pete, who scratched him for his efforts. Jeremy felt a blaze of anger. Immediately, Tiamat tensed her legs, as if to launch herself at the cat.

NO! he thought.

Tiamat sent her question feeling.

He tried to explain that Pete was just lashing out because he was angry. He wasn't sure he got the point across, but it gave Pete time to get away.

Jeremy picked up his books. Still smarting from Freddy's kick, he pushed his way out of the bushes and limped home.

Rather than going into the house, Jeremy headed for his father's office. *Hold still,* he thought to Tiamat. *I want to get something to put on your wings.*

The dragon sent back a message of agreement.

Dr. Thatcher whistled when his son walked through the door. "What happened to you?" he asked. "You look like you've been dancing with Fat Pete."

Jeremy blinked in astonishment. Could his father possibly know what had just happened?

"What do you mean?" he asked nervously.

"Those scratches," said Dr. Thatcher. "I hope Mary Lou didn't do that to you."

Jeremy put his hand to his cheek. He had been so worried about Tiamat and Fat Pete that he hadn't noticed what had happened to his own face when he fell.

"Do you want some ointment for . . . " Dr. Thatcher's voice trailed off. He looked at Jeremy and blinked.

"Dad?"

Dr. Thatcher shook his head. "I've been working too hard," he said, rubbing a hand across his eyes.

Jeremy sighed. For a moment he thought his father had started to see Tiamat. Life would be so much easier if he knew about her. For a moment he considered trying to tell his father. But he remembered Mr. Elives' letter. By accepting the dragon, he had accepted a vow of secrecy.

"Let me get those cleaned up," said Dr. Thatcher, pointing to the scratches on Jeremy's face. "Then I want to put some ointment on them. Only don't tell your mother! She doesn't like it when I use animal medicine on you, even if it is perfectly good."

Jeremy sighed. One more secret to keep. "Is this

stuff good for *any* animal?" he asked as his father smeared the salve on his scratches.

"All-purpose antiseptic," said Dr. Thatcher. "Guaranteed to zap germs before they can get a foothold."

"Can I have some extra?" asked Jeremy.

Dr. Thatcher hesitated. "Sure," he said, staring again at the place where Tiamat perched on Jeremy's shoulder. He closed his eyes and then opened them. "Take all you want."

When he entered the house Jeremy found a letter waiting for him on the dining room table. The spidery handwriting on the envelope was the same as that on the magic shop's direction sheet.

He waited until he had smoothed salve over Tiamat's wings. Then, feeling nervous, he opened the envelope. His fingers trembled as he unfolded the crisp paper. The words it held were both a relief and the worst thing he could possibly imagine.

Thatcher:

It will soon be time for the dragon to go home. Come to the corner of Main and Not Main at 11:30 on Midsummer Night. Bring the dragon, as well as any teeth it has lost, any skins it has shed, and whatever bits of eggshell you were able to save.

Be prompt!

S. H. Elives

Jeremy stared at the note in distress. He had always guessed that Tiamat would have to go home sooner or later. Part of him had even been eager for that to happen; certainly life would be simpler without a dragon to care for.

But another part of him had hidden from the idea. He had never really prepared himself to cope with the thought of her leaving. He had let himself grow used to her sendings, her questions, her constant presence in his head. Now the very thought of losing her made a great wave of loneliness well within him. As it did, he found his head filled with an image of dragons—hundreds of dragons, flying through a darkened sky.

Home! sang a feeling inside him.

He blinked, and the image vanished.

Jeremy looked at Tiamat.

Home! she repeated—not in words, of course, but by sending him a feeling which could mean nothing else.

Late that night Jeremy was tiptoeing up the stairs with some chicken livers for Tiamat. Suddenly his mother stepped into the hallway, tightening the belt on her robe. She looked at the plate in his hand and said, "What are you doing?"

"I . . . uh . . . I'm doing an experiment. You know—how feeding meat to an animal compares with just giving it pellets and stuff."

Mrs. Thatcher closed her eyes. "You're trying to create killer gerbils? Does your father know about this?"

Jeremy shook his head.

"Well, check with him. He's been wondering where his chicken livers have been going. I don't think he'll be too happy to find out you're using them to play mad scientist."

"I'll talk to him about it tomorrow," promised Jeremy.

Mrs. Thatcher nodded, then walked into the bathroom. Jeremy waited until she had closed the door, then dashed for his own room. He found Tiamat crouched in the middle of the floor, trying to breathe flame.

Stop that! thought Jeremy, as he put the livers in front of her. *You'll scorch the floor!*

I want to make fire! thought Tiamat, as she started to gobble the livers.

Do you suppose you could cut back on those? asked Jeremy. *I think I'm going to have to start buying them out of my allowance.*

Tiamat sent an image of a plateful of gerbils, lying on their backs, their little paws stiff above them.

"Forget it," said Jeremy. "I'll buy the chicken livers!"

A red-and-gold sigh trickled through his head as the dragon returned her attention to her meal.

The next morning, Jeremy found Tiamat sitting on his desk, preening her burnished scales. Lying beside her was another discarded skin. Her tail, which hung over the edge of the desk, reached nearly to the floor.

Jeremy rolled the crinkly red skin and put it with the others. As he did, he wondered again how big she was going to get.

BIG! replied Tiamat cheerfully.

Too big for this room, thought Jeremy, stroking her head—which was now wider than his fist, and longer than his foot. In fact, if she continued to grow at this rate, it wouldn't be long before she would no longer fit through the door. He wished he could get a little of that growing ability for himself.

What am I going to do with you? he thought.

Tiamat curved her neck around his arm. *Send me home,* she replied, in a combination of pictures and feelings.

Jeremy's stomach tightened. When he had gone to bed last night, he had considered ignoring the summons that had come from the magic shop. When Midsummer Night (whatever that was) came, he would just stay right here with Tiamat. The idea had been a little frightening—but not as frightening as losing the dragon.

But if she *wanted* to go—well, that was different. He couldn't keep her here against her will.

A wave of sadness, muddy green and dark brown, rolled through him. He understood. Tiamat didn't want to go. Not entirely. But she knew she had to.

But where. Where was home?

Well, he knew one place where he might find an answer: Miss Priest's book. He could sense Tiamat's approval when he took it to his desk and began to read.

"Listen to this," he said after a while.

Tiamat closed her eyes and listened while he read from the book.

> The time came when this world was no longer safe for dragons. Earth had too many heroes, too many swords—and not enough magic. One by one, the great dragons were being slaughtered.
>
> In an attempt to save the last dragons, the wizard Bellenmore opened a door between the worlds. Through this gate, the remaining dragons passed to the new world that was to be their home.
>
> It was a harsh world, but it was a world without men, and therefore safer for dragons.
>
> Yet, as things turned out, there was still a problem. Suited as this world was to the great beasts, it was unfit for their eggs. Though many eggs were laid, for over a hundred years, not one new egg hatched. Dragons live for a tremendous time, of course, but during the second century of this blight, they began to fear that their kind would become extinct after all.
>
> Finally the dragons contacted Bellenmore's successor, Aaron the Wise (later known as Aaron Dragonfriend), and requested his aid.
>
> Aaron brought a dragon's egg home with him, to see if it could be hatched here in the

world where dragons had once lived. He discovered that without our moon to quicken it, a dragon's egg remains dormant forever. With this knowledge, he was able to hatch the egg. Later, when the dragon had grown too large to stay here safely, Aaron faced great peril to send it back to the rest of its kind.

This was the beginning of the Company of Hatchers. Since that first hatching, a handful of eggs have come to this world each decade. Each egg is held out of sight of the moon, until the right person appears. Then the egg is entrusted to the Hatcher, who must guard the young dragon and, when the time is right, help it to go home.

Jeremy closed the book and sighed. It looked like he had better find out about Midsummer Night.

ELEVEN

Confessions

"Ah, Midsummer Night," said Mr. Thatcher. "Wonderful date, filled with magic. Twenty-third of June, if I remember correctly."

"That's not the *middle* of summer," cried Jeremy. "It's the beginning!"

"Just another little trick of the English language," said Dr. Thatcher with a shrug.

Jeremy felt sick. He had thought Tiamat would still be with him for another couple of months. Midsummer Night wasn't nearly so far away.

"Anything wrong?" asked Dr. Thatcher.

Jeremy shook his head and left the room. For some reason June 23rd sounded vaguely familiar. He went to check the calendar in the kitchen and found that the date was circled. He had circled it himself, in red, with exclamation points, because it was the last day of school for the year. And it was only two weeks away.

Two weeks, thought Jeremy in despair. *Can I stand to let Tiamat go, when the time comes?*

He really didn't know. The dragon was a part of him now. He was used to her constant presence in his mind, the never-absent play of colors at the back of his head that spoke to him of her moods. He loved those colors. They were starting to show up in his art, making it richer and stronger than it had ever been before.

Yet Tiamat was already too big to stay in his room. In fact, he was planning to move her to one of the small barns that very night.

Jeremy waited until the house was quiet. Walking on tiptoe, he led Tiamat down the stairs. Though the cats hissed as they crossed the kitchen, none of them came near. Jeremy had to open the door for Tiamat. The cat door she had been able to slip through such a short time ago was already far too small for her.

"Now for heaven's sake, don't sit in here and try to breathe flame," said Jeremy as he led Tiamat into the barn. "You'll burn the whole place down!"

He accompanied the speech with an image of a flame-breathing Tiamat setting the barn on fire, and a sense of how upset he would be if that happened.

Don't worry, she replied with a whirl of white and gold.

After Tiamat was settled into one of the abandoned stalls, Jeremy returned to his room—and worried. He worried so much that the next day in school, somewhat to his own surprise, he found himself telling Mary Lou both that Tiamat had grown enormously large, and that she was supposed to leave.

"What are you going to do?" asked Mary Lou.

"What *can* I do? She can't stay here."

Mary Lou put her hand on his arm. "Do you want me to go with you when you take her?" she asked quietly.

Jeremy surprised himself again by considering the offer.

"I don't think so," he said at last. "Saying goodbye to her is something I'm going to have to do on my own."

"There must be some way I can help you."

Jeremy shrugged. "You can help feed her if you want."

Mary Lou seemed delighted. "I'll bring over a gallon of milk tomorrow morning!"

In fact, Mary Lou rode her bike over with a gallon of milk every day that week. On Friday morning, Jeremy began to wonder if the milk trick was still working. That was because Fat Pete's owner came to the Thatcher house to ask if anyone had seen his cat.

Jeremy swallowed hard. Though Fat Pete often wandered away, he always came back within a day or two. Now he had been gone for three days—the exact amount of time Tiamat had been in the barn. Had he saved the cranky cat from Freddy only to have Tiamat down it for a midnight snack?

Excusing himself, he raced down to the barn.

Tiamat was waiting, her long neck stretched out beyond the edge of the stall.

Breakfast? she asked, sending an image of her bucket of milk, along with her question feeling.

"Later," said Jeremy irritably. Then he sent her an image of Fat Pete, along with his own question feeling.

The feeling she sent back could best be translated as *Yum!*

Jeremy turned pale. Did that mean that she had eaten the cat—or only that she would like to?

He was still trying to figure out how to image the question when Mary Lou walked in with a gallon of milk.

"Good grief," she said, staring at Tiamat in awe. "She's getting bigger by the day."

Jeremy nodded in dismay. Judging by the marks he had been making on the stall wall, she was at least a foot longer than yesterday. Most of that was tail, but still, her size was getting to be a matter of real concern. Much as he loved her, Tiamat at ten feet was not as charming as Tiamat at ten inches.

"Do you think this will be enough?" asked Mary Lou, as she poured the milk into Tiamat's plastic bucket.

"I sure hope so," said Jeremy. Then he told her about Fat Pete.

"You don't know that Tiamat did it," said Mary Lou defensively.

"True," said Jeremy. "But I don't know that she didn't, either." He shivered. "What if she goes on

a binge some night and eats all my father's patients?"

"Maybe I'd better go back and get some more milk," said Mary Lou. She looked embarrassed. "Only, I'm out of money."

Jeremy dug in his jeans. "The way things are going, I'm going to have to find a job just to feed her," he said ruefully, handing Mary Lou the last of his allowance.

They left for school with no clear answer to the question of Fat Pete.

When they passed the Bothill house, Specimen moped out to join them. He was the only boy in the class who would still walk with Jeremy, now that Jeremy was walking to and from school with Mary Lou.

"I wish whoever gave Kravitz that hotfoot would confess," said Specimen.

Jeremy felt himself blush. "Wasn't it worth missing the contest to see Mr. Kravitz get that hotfoot?" he asked hopefully.

Specimen shrugged. "No one asked if I was willing to give up the contest for the sake of a laugh."

Jeremy's stomach grew tight. It wasn't fair for Spess to be punished for something Tiamat had done. But the only way he could change that would be to tell Mr. Kravitz that he was the one who had given him the hotfoot.

In a way, he wished that he had.

Jeremy thought about it all morning. At noon he went to Mr. Sigel and said, "May I go see Mr. Kravitz for a few minutes?

Mr. Sigel raised an eyebrow, then shrugged. "If you want to," he said.

Jeremy was relieved that he didn't ask why. But that was one of the things he liked about Mr. Sigel. Even though he made a lot of suggestions, he never pried into your personal life.

Jeremy's hands began to tremble as he walked to the artroom.

Are you all right?

Tiamat's question whispered through his brain in a mist of blue and yellow.

Yes! he thought fiercely.

She returned an image of his shaking hands, along with her question feeling.

I have something to do, thought Jeremy. *Something difficult.* He tried to think of a picture to explain, but couldn't.

Shall I come help you?

NO!

Tiamat broke the connection, but not before sending a message of puzzled dismay.

Great, thought Jeremy. *If there's anything left of me after I'm done with Mr. Kravitz, I get to deal with a dragon in a snit. How do I get myself into these situations?*

When Jeremy entered the art room he found Mr. Kravitz sitting at one of the long tables, drawing. The teacher didn't notice him right away, so Jeremy stood and watched the man work.

Finally Mr. Kravitz looked up. "Thatcher," he said, in such a neutral way that Jeremy couldn't tell if it was a greeting, a statement, or a question.

Even so, he could feel his stomach getting still tighter.

"Well, what is it?" asked Mr. Kravitz.

Jeremy swallowed hard. "I'm the one who gave you that hotfoot."

"Nice try, Thatcher," said Mr. Kravitz. His voice had a note of contempt. He returned to his drawing.

"Nice try?" asked Jeremy, uncertain what that meant.

Mr. Kravitz put down his pencil. "You didn't give me that hotfoot, and we both know it. You were too far away. Who are you protecting? That little weasel, Freddy? What did he do, threaten to hit you if you didn't take the blame?"

Jeremy blinked in confusion. He had confessed, and the confession had been rejected. Now what was he supposed to do? Explain that it was actually his dragon that had done the deed?

His throat hurt. His stomach was a knot of emotion. Years of frustration seethed within him. Before he realized what he was doing, he said, "Mr. Kravitz, why do you hate me?"

Mr. Kravitz looked at him in astonishment. Jeremy blinked at his own boldness; frightened, he took a step back. As he did, he noticed Mr. Kravitz's hand begin to twitch. Suddenly the art teacher seemed to notice it, too. He looked at his hand, put down the pencil, and then looked back at Jeremy, who saw something terrible in the man's eyes—a kind of anger, but a sadness, too.

When Mr. Kravitz finally spoke, his voice was little more than a whisper. "Do you really believe that I hate you?" he asked.

Jeremy hesitated. Probably he should just say no, and let it go. But he had come too far now to drop the matter. He had put the truth as he felt it in the open. He had to stand by it. Summoning all his courage, he looked back at Mr. Kravitz and nodded.

The big man turned away for a moment. When he turned back, his face was twisted, as if he were in pain. "I think you are the most talented student I have ever taught," he said slowly. "Talented, but undisciplined. You need them both, Thatcher. Talent and discipline. One without the other is useless."

Jeremy stared at him in astonishment. Mr. Kravitz stared back. Uncomfortable, Jeremy lowered his eyes to the picture Mr. Kravitz had been working on, a stiff drawing of some trees beside a pond. The drawing was accurate, but still and lifeless. As he watched, Mr. Kravitz's big fingers twitched. The drawing crumpled beneath them.

Suddenly it all came clear to Jeremy. Mr. Kravitz *didn't* hate him. The problem was that the man was jealous—jealous because Jeremy was a better artist than he was.

The idea was astonishing. It couldn't be true.

Or could it?

Maybe what Mr. Kravitz resented—hated, even—was that he, Jeremy, was talented, but didn't show any discipline.

He returned his gaze to the teacher's face, searching it for information.

The big man looked away from him. "Who really gave me that hotfoot?" he asked after a moment.

"I was responsible," said Jeremy truthfully.

Mr. Kravitz sighed. "Go back to your room," he said. "Your class is back in the contest. Everyone except you."

TWELVE

Night Flights

"I've got a chance!" shouted Specimen when he heard the news. He was so excited, he raced home to work on his entry as soon as school was over.

Jeremy stayed behind, thinking about his conversation with Mr. Kravitz. He had told Spess only half of it. The personal part—the stuff about his own talent—he was keeping to himself.

Normally he would have told Specimen everything. But lately he hadn't felt like talking to Spess so much. That shout of joy hadn't done anything to help matters. It was clear Specimen considered Jeremy's banishment from the contest fair punishment for getting the class in trouble to begin with.

Jeremy was sick of it all—the teasing, the punishment, the injustice. He broke his favorite drawing pencil in half and threw it into the wastebasket.

By the time he left the building the only kid still hanging around was Mary Lou. She was waiting for him on the steps of the school.

"That was a nice thing you did," she said.

"I don't want to talk about it."

Mary Lou started to say something else, then changed her mind. "We've got company," she said, switching the topic altogether.

Jeremy looked around warily. Were Howard and Freddy waiting to pound him?

"Wrong direction," said Mary Lou. "Look up."

He did, turning in a slow circle, until he spotted Tiamat looming on the edge of the school roof. She was staring down at him with a look that could only be the dragon version of a smile. The tip of her tail dangled down so far it nearly reached the windows.

What are you doing here? he demanded.

I came to take you home.

Before Jeremy could ask what she meant, Tiamat leapt from the roof, spread her wings and began to glide toward him, her claws extended before her.

"Tiamat!" he yelled. "Tiamat, don't!"

"What's going on?" cried Mary Lou.

Jeremy's reply was cut short when Tiamat grabbed him by his sides and snatched him into the air. Jeremy's stomach lurched as the world fell away beneath them.

"Put me down!" he cried "Put me down!" But Tiamat only pumped her wings harder.

Hold still! she commanded when he started to squirm. She sent him an image of a wriggling body falling from a great height.

He held still.

Now look. Look!

Jeremy looked. The world that spread below him was beautiful—more beautiful than he had ever imagined. He had no idea Blodgett's Crossing had so many trees; it was greener than he would have guessed.

I love this place, he thought with surprise.

It's your home, replied Tiamat, as she carried him over the park.

He enjoyed the flight until he spotted a pair of familiar figures below.

Watch out, he sent nervously, *I see Howard and Freddy.*

He could feel Tiamat's amusement. *They can't see you,* she told him, using the same kind of images she had used to explain why his mother hadn't seen her. Jeremy wondered if that meant he was invisible while she carried him. He liked the idea.

The flight was the greatest adventure of his life, and Jeremy couldn't wait to repeat it.

That night, after everyone was asleep, he slipped out of the house and walked down to the barn. Tiamat was waiting for him.

Let me try riding, he thought, sending a picture of himself mounted on her back.

Tiamat agreed, and Jeremy found it far more comfortable to straddle her back than to be carried in her claws. Once he was settled, she pumped her

great wings, and they lifted into the moonlit sky. Jeremy waited until they were several hundred feet above the earth to let out a shout of joy.

Every night after that, Jeremy slipped out of the house at midnight to accompany the dragon on her journeys across the sky. Sometimes she went so high that the air became thin and hard to breathe. They flew into clouds, skimmed across rivers, soared over cliffs.

Tiamat hunted on these nights. Out in the wild, away from the pets and people of the town, she would put Jeremy on top of a high hill and then swoop through the darkness, catching squirrels, rabbits, bats, and raccoons.

The first time he watched her eat a rabbit he thought he was going to be sick. *No sense in getting mad at a dragon for being a dragon,* he told himself, turning his head from the gory sight.

But even the hunting she was doing was not enough. She was over twenty feet long now, and still growing. Soon she would need larger prey.

I have to go home soon, Tiamat told him each night when the flight was over. Jeremy would nod, leaning his head against her shoulder, trying not to weep. Once she folded a leathery wing around his shoulder, as if embracing him.

Yet as much as he dreaded her leaving, he knew it would also be a relief. Caring for her had put such a strain on him that his mother had started to worry about his health. A week after the night rides began, Mrs. Thatcher announced she was taking him to the doctor for a checkup.

"Why can't Dad check me?" protested Jeremy. "He's a doctor."

"He's a veterinarian!" said Mrs. Thatcher crossly. "I want you to see a people doctor." But other than general exhaustion, Dr. Hulan found nothing wrong with Jeremy.

"Have you been getting enough sleep?" he asked, rubbing his bearded chin in puzzlement.

When Jeremy shook his head, Dr. Hulan scowled. "Start sending him to bed earlier," he said to Mrs. Thatcher. "And give him a mug of warm milk before he turns in."

That was fine with Jeremy. He had been looking for an excuse to go to bed early. A little extra sleep then would give him more energy for his midnight flights with Tiamat.

Not that there were many of them left.

Soon, far too soon, Friday the 23rd of June arrived.

The day of Midsummer Night was a day of endings—the last day not only of school, but of sixth grade. Jeremy had gone to Blodgett's Crossing Elementary more than half his life. Leaving it with the thought that next year he would go someplace new was both exciting and frightening.

The school gathered for a final awards assembly. When Mr. Martinez announced that Specimen had won first prize in the art contest Jeremy clapped and cheered. But inside he ached, because he had wanted so much to win it himself. He wondered if Spess would remember their mutual pledge that the winner would share the prize.

Jeremy was leaving the building, still stinging with loss, when Mr. Kravitz stopped him.

"Thatcher," he said.

Jeremy turned. His stomach grew tight with the anticipation of something nasty about to happen.

Mr. Kravitz paused. Then to Jeremy's surprise, he nodded and said, "Good luck next year."

What was even more amazing was that he sounded like he meant it.

But even that miracle did little to distract him from the coming loss, and he spent the afternoon in a daze of sorrow.

After dinner, he placed Tiamat's baby teeth in a small leather bag his uncle had given him several years before. He had found nearly three dozen of them, the tiniest no larger than a pencil point, the biggest nearly the size of his little finger. Their soft, pearly color disguised the fact that they were razor sharp and steel hard.

Next he took her skins—she had shed seven times in all—out to the barn. When he had smoothed them out on the floor they were like a diary of Tiamat's growth. He laid the first skin, barely a foot long, in the palm of his hand. It reminded him of the night she had hatched.

I was tiny! she sent, the message a combination of a crystal-clear image of the hatching, accompanied by a gentle sense of amusement.

I was frightened, he replied.

Remembering that night made him remember the magic shop, and something Mr. Elives had said to him.

Did you really choose me? he asked.

She replied with a flood of warm assurance.

Why?

I liked the colors in your head. I knew we could share beautiful pictures. She poked her head, which was as big as a horse's, over his shoulder. *I will miss you.*

And I will miss you, replied Jeremy, stroking her scaly nose. Beneath her eye he felt a piece of hard material. It came away in his fingertips. When he held it up, it sparkled in the light.

What is this?

Dragons weep diamonds, replied Tiamat, turning her head away.

Jeremy pressed the tear to his chest. In the distance he could hear his mother calling him to come in. He glanced at his watch. Almost bedtime.

Placing Tiamat's skins one on top of the other, he rolled them up, then tied the crinkly red bundle with a strand of yarn he had found in his mother's knitting bag. Next to it he placed the box in which he had carried home Tiamat's egg. Inside, saved as per the directions, were the pieces of the shell. Next to that, he set the bag of teeth.

Jeremy looked at the collection of material—the box, the bag and the scroll—and wondered if he should add Tiamat's tear. But the letter hadn't mentioned anything about this, so brushing away a tear of his own, he tucked the gem into his pocket.

When he turned to go, he saw Mary Lou Hutton standing in the doorway.

"I came to say good-bye to Tiamat," she said softly.

Jeremy nodded.

Mary Lou walked to the dragon. "Farewell, Lady Tiamat," she whispered.

Tiamat dipped her long neck, and Mary Lou embraced her.

After a moment she turned to Jeremy and asked, as she had several times over the last few days, "Do you want me to come tonight?"

He shook his head. "I have to do this alone," he replied, as always.

Mary Lou nodded. "Good luck," she whispered. Her voice was husky; he could tell that she felt nearly as bad as he did.

Shortly after eleven o'clock, Jeremy tiptoed out of his room carrying the box, the scroll, the bag of teeth, and a flashlight. With no Tiamat to intimidate them, the kitchen cats rubbed around his ankles, begging for a late-night treat. Ignoring their pleas, Jeremy slipped out the back door.

The night was cool and still, without a breath of wind, almost as if it were waiting for something to happen.

Jeremy didn't need to walk to the barn; having sensed his approach, Tiamat was waiting for him in the yard. In the silvery light of the full moon she looked enormous.

They started walking. It would have been easier to fly, of course. Only they couldn't, because Jeremy had no idea where they were going. That wasn't for lack of trying; two days earlier he had walked the entire length of Main Street looking for the corner of "Main and Not Main." As far as he could tell, it didn't exist. That didn't surprise him. He had lived in Blodgett's Crossing all his life and never heard of such an intersection. But its absence had worried him. How was he supposed to take the dragon to a corner that wasn't there?

Finally he had decided they would just walk along Main Street and see what happened. If the old man wanted them, odds were good that he would find them.

They were less than a block from home when Jeremy heard a car. He dove for the bushes. No telling what would happen if someone spotted him wandering around at this time of night!

Maybe you should ride on my back, suggested Tiamat. *Then no one will be able to see you.*

She crouched down, and Jeremy climbed on. In a way, it felt even stranger to ride on a dragon walking through town than to fly with her.

The air was cool and moist, and as they neared the center of town fog began to creep toward them. It grew rapidly thicker. By the time they were two blocks past the main intersection, Jeremy could hardly see.

Too bad we don't know where the corner is, thought Jeremy to Tiamat. *Then we could fly, instead of walking through this stuff.*

She sent her agreement.

The fog got still thicker, curling around Tiamat's feet like snakes made of smoke. Jeremy begin to worry again. He had a feeling that if they continued walking, they really would come to the corner of "Main and Not Main."

But when we do, will we be in Blodgett's Crossing—or somewhere else altogether?

The fog seemed to muffle the sound of Tiamat's footsteps. Jeremy felt as if he and Tiamat were the only things moving through the silence and the darkness.

Finally he slid off her back and asked her to fly ahead to see if she could see anything. She hadn't been gone more than a few seconds when he felt a great sense of isolation sweep over him. *Come back!* he thought desperately.

He could feel Tiamat wheel above him. The rush of her wings as she landed made the fog swirl in a way that was almost angry.

Nasty, she sent.

Jeremy put his hand on her scaly neck, and they walked on. No need to ride her now. No one could see him through this stuff.

Soon the fog was so dense that even with the flashlight Jeremy couldn't see more than a few feet ahead. The flashlight was still helpful, though, because if he stood right at the base of a street sign, the beam reached just far enough for him to read the name.

After they passed Oak, Ash, and Willow, something strange began to happen. They started to cross streets he had never heard of before—streets with names like Wand, Staff, and Stave.

Two blocks past Stave, Jeremy thought they had found the corner they were seeking. He wasn't sure, because there was no street sign—only a narrow dirt path that led into a thick forest. The thing was, there were no dirt paths crossing Main Street . . . and no forests in Blodgett's Crossing.

"Mr. Elives?" called Jeremy.

His voice seemed to vanish in the mist.

"Mr. Elives?"

No answer.

He pointed the flashlight at his watch. As the second hand swept up to make 11:30 on the dot, a hooded figure stepped from the mist. Jeremy swallowed. The newcomer was tall—much taller than the old man he had met in the shop.

He was about to run when the figure reached up and pulled back its hood.

Jeremy blinked. "What are *you* doing here?" he asked in astonishment.

THIRTEEN

Nothing You Love Is Lost

It was Miss Priest, the librarian. She wore a crown of daisies in her hair. She stared at Jeremy, and he saw something terrible in her eyes, fierce and sad and angry all at the same time.

"Greetings, Hatcher," she said. "Did you bring the teeth?"

Jeremy nodded and held up the bag. Then, thinking that Miss Priest might not be able to see him in the darkness, he whispered, "Yes."

"And the skins?"

"Yes. And the eggshells."

Miss Priest murmured her approval, then turned to Tiamat and made a deep curtsy. "And how are you tonight, milady?"

To Jeremy's astonishment, Tiamat raised her head and shot a line of flame fifteen feet into the sky.

"Indeed!" said Miss Priest. She sounded impressed. She turned to Jeremy and whispered. "You have done well."

"Thank you."

For a moment, no one said anything else. Finally Jeremy asked, "What happens next?"

"You may go home if you wish," replied Miss Priest. "Your job is finished."

Jeremy looked at her in shock. Just like that, it was over? He handed his dragon to a strange woman on a dark corner, and that was the end of it? "I don't want to go home," he said.

"Then if you are feeling brave, you may come with me."

Jeremy swallowed. He wasn't feeling brave at all. But neither did he feel like just letting go of Tiamat.

"Where are we going?"

"To a place you've already been."

"The mag—"

She pressed a finger to his lips, warning him to silence. "Careful, Hatcher," she whispered. "This is a strange night, and words have more power than you think, even under the best of circumstances. Try not to use them unnecessarily."

Jeremy nodded.

"Turn off your flashlight."

He did as she asked. Miss Priest took his hand and led him into the darkness. The mist was damp against his face. It wove about the trunks of the trees, gleaming silver in the moonlight. The night was oddly silent, as if the darkness were swallowing all sound, even that of his footsteps. When he looked behind him to be sure that Tiamat was still there, he could see her green eyes glowing in the dark.

No need to look, she informed him. *You can tell if I'm here.*

Jeremy nodded. Even if she couldn't see the gesture, he knew she would sense his response.

After a while he could see a light through the fog. As they drew closer, Jeremy saw that it came from the magic shop. But the store was not sitting at the end of a street, as he had first seen it. It was in a forest clearing.

Jeremy swallowed nervously.

The door swung open as they approached. Miss Priest entered first. Jeremy followed. Tiamat came last, tucking her wings against her sides. When Jeremy turned to watch, he had a sense that the door was stretching itself to let her pass. He blinked, and she was in.

The hoot of an owl made him look to the back of the store.

"Greetings," said Mr. Elives. He shuffled across the floor, stopping in front of Tiamat, who took up most of the available space. He examined the dragon for a few moments, then turned to Jeremy and said, "It appears that you have done a good job."

"Thank you."

"What is her spoken name?"

"Tiamat."

Mr. Elives snorted. "The Queen of the Universe! Well, her line always did have a streak of vanity. Of course, that's not her real name. She can't tell you that."

Jeremy felt a twinge of jealousy. Did the old man know her real name?

Mr. Elives turned to Miss Priest. She had moved to one of the counters, where she was unrolling the skins Jeremy had brought. "How is that coming?" he asked.

"It will be ready," said Miss Priest, without looking up. "You'd best see to your part."

Muttering to himself, Mr. Elives gestured to the dragon, and then shuffled out of the room.

Folding her wings and pulling in her sides so she could get around the counter, Tiamat followed.

Jeremy started after her, but Miss Priest put a hand on his shoulder. "Stay here," she whispered.

Jeremy jumped. He had thought she was still at the counter.

When Miss Priest saw that he wasn't going to argue, she returned to her work. After a bit, Jeremy walked over to see what she was doing. As he watched, she began matching the teeth he had brought with some pieces of dark wood.

"Why are you doing that?"

"I'm going to make a gate." She picked up one of the teeth and inserted it into a notch that had been carved in the end of one of the sticks. "You may help if you wish," she said, without looking at him.

Jeremy thought he caught a hint of challenge

in her voice. He hesitated. Helping her build a gate to send Tiamat to another world felt a little like helping to weave a rope for his own hanging. But it was better than standing around and feeling helpless. "What do I do?" he asked.

Miss Priest picked up one of the sticks. It was about as long as her index finger, and slightly thinner than a pencil. "See this notch?" she said, pointing to one end of the stick. "You slide the tooth in like this."

As she spoke, she inserted a small tooth in the stick. The tooth, which was wide at the base, tapered to a wicked point. The base fit snugly into the notch. At first, Jeremy thought the combination of stick and tooth looked like a little spear. Then he noticed the hole drilled through the other end of the stick, and decided that the whole thing looked more like a big needle.

"You try," said Miss Priest.

Jeremy picked up one of the smaller teeth. But when he tried to slide it into a stick, his hand slipped, and he jabbed the tooth into his own palm. It disappeared into the flesh. Crying out, he pressed his thumb against the wound to stop the bleeding.

"That was an interesting thing to do," said Miss Priest. "We'll have to check to make sure we still have enough."

Jeremy watched her spread the remaining sticks and teeth across the counter. Wasn't she going to offer him a bandage or something?

Miss Priest matched the sticks to the teeth.

"Good," she said. "We have just the right number."

"What about this?" asked Jeremy, moving his thumb to show her his cut.

Miss Priest looked at him. "What about it?"

Jeremy glanced at his hand. The wound was gone. All that remained to show what had happened was a smear of drying blood and a short white line where the tooth had entered his skin.

"Done!" said Miss Priest, setting the last tooth into the last stick. "Though I can't say you were much help."

Despite the chiding words, her face was still and calm.

She reached for one of the skins. As she spread it in front of her, she turned over her right hand. In the center of her palm Jeremy saw a white line that looked exactly like the new mark in his own hand. He blinked. But when he started to ask her about it, Miss Priest shook her head and placed a finger against her lips. She tipped her head toward the back of the shop, where Mr. Elives had gone, then shook it once more.

Each gesture was small and silent. Jeremy's head swirled with the sense of secrets within secrets. He felt trapped between powers that he didn't understand.

Miss Priest turned her hand away from him. Pulling a bit of eggshell from the box, she used its sharp edge to cut the skin in a spiral shape.

"You see?" she said, as she threaded a strip of

the skin through one of the needles they had made. "Shell, skin, and tooth all work together. They are all supposed to go back to her world. Nothing should remain here."

"I don't want Tiamat to go back," said Jeremy sullenly. "I want her to stay here with me."

Miss Priest laughed. It was not a horrible laugh at all. "What a terrible idea!" she said. "Why do you want her to stay?"

"Because I love her. I don't want to lose her."

Miss Priest reached out and took his chin in her hand. She looked into his eyes. "You silly boy," she said. "Nothing you love is lost. Not really. Things, people—they always go away, sooner or later. You can't hold them, any more than you can hold moonlight. But if they've touched you, if they're inside you, then they're still yours. The only things you ever really have are the ones you hold inside your heart."

She turned away from him and lowered her head. Then she crossed her hands over her chest and whispered:

> Full moon's light to wake the egg,
> Full moon's light to hatch it;
> Midsummer Night will break your heart
> All Hallow's Eve may patch it.

Jeremy recognized the poem; it was the one he had recited on the night he hatched the egg.

Or is it? It seems different, somehow.

Before he could work out what had changed, Mr. Elives came back. "It's nearly time," he said softly.

Jeremy looked at his watch. Five minutes till midnight.

"Where's Tiamat?" he asked.

Mr. Elives nodded toward the back of the shop. But when Jeremy started in that direction, the old man put out a hand to stop him.

"I have to tell her good-bye," said Jeremy.

Mr. Elives shook his head. "You can't go back there."

"But I didn't tell her good-bye. I didn't tell her I love her."

Before Mr. Elives could refuse him again, Miss Priest put her hand on the old man's arm. "Let the boy in," she said.

The old man snorted, but shrugged.

Jeremy passed beyond the curtain, into a place unlike anything he had ever seen before. The walls, if they were walls, seemed to be made of nothing but mist. A dim light suffused the area. In the middle crouched Tiamat. She looked frightened.

Jeremy was frightened, too. Frightened by the strangeness of the place, by what he knew was about to happen. But he could not turn back. Crossing to Tiamat, he put his arms about her neck and laid his head against hers.

I shall miss you so, he told her.

She nodded, and sent him an image of a crystal breaking in half.

"Now step away," said Mr. Elives crossly.

"I love you, Tiamat," whispered Jeremy. He stumbled back and watched as Miss Priest and Mr. Elives assembled the sticks and the strips of skin into a circle on the ground. They scattered the bits of eggshell across it. Mr. Elives gestured, and the circle tipped up, until it formed a glowing gate. The bits of eggshell floated within the circle, shining like distant stars.

"The time has come, milady," said Miss Priest softly.

Tiamat stepped forward. Jeremy could feel her slipping away from him. He closed his eyes. *Don't go!* he thought desperately. *Don't go!*

Suddenly Jeremy felt like he was being torn in half. He cried out. As he did, he heard an answering squeal of pain. Opening his eyes he saw an awful sight. Tiamat, half in the circle and half out, was shaking with terrible spasms. Light sparked and flashed around her.

"Something's holding her!" cried Miss Priest.

Mr. Elives turned to Jeremy. "Let her go, you little fool!" he shouted. "Let her go!"

Miss Priest ran to Jeremy's side. "Let her go, Hatcher," she cried. "She'll die, trapped between two worlds. If you love her, you have to *let her go*."

A great sob tore from Jeremy's throat. *Go!* he thought. *Go home!*

And then it was over. Tiamat was gone, and the place where they stood was plunged into darkness.

Miss Priest wrapped Jeremy in her cloak and guided him back into the shop.

"The side door will get you home more quickly," she said. Then, bending close to his ear, she whispered, "Be brave, Dragon Hatcher. Nothing you love is ever really lost."

Jeremy barely realized he had left the shop, until he found himself only a few blocks from home. The fog was gone, the full moon once more clear in the sky.

A warm wind whispered around him and the leaves overhead rustled with secrets. Jeremy didn't listen. Moaning, he stumbled to a tree and pressed his head against it.

Tiamat was gone.

Clutching the rough bark, he began to sob.

Epilogue

The summer dragged by in a blur of emptiness. Jeremy watched Specimen paint the window of Zambreno's Department Store. Although Specimen invited him to help, Jeremy couldn't bring himself to lift a brush. He hadn't done a bit of art since Midsummer Night.

Fat Pete returned in July, wearing a new scar and crankier than ever.

Howard and Freddy whispered to each other whenever they saw Jeremy in the park. But they stayed away from him, as they had ever since Jeremy and Tiamat had chased Freddy away.

Mary Lou, who gave up trying to talk to him, watched with sorrowful eyes as he moved further and further into himself.

His parents grew increasingly worried. When his mother asked, "Why don't you draw anymore, sweetheart?" as she did on several occasions, Jeremy only shrugged. He didn't know how to explain; he couldn't even explain it to himself.

He did not go back to the library, either. He didn't want to see Miss Priest. Not that he blamed her for the loss of Tiamat—at least, not much. He just didn't want to see her.

In August she sent him a note, telling him he could have the book she had loaned him. "It's not a library book," she wrote. "Rather, it is from my private collection. Keep it, as a thank-you for your efforts."

He thought often of the words she had whispered to him the night that Tiamat left. "Midsummer Night will break your heart, All Hallow's Eve may patch it."

What was that supposed to mean, anyway? Time heals everything? Big deal. He knew he would get over this, sooner or later. In a way. But nothing could convince him that life would ever be the same as it had been when he had had a dragon.

Summer came to an end. He started seventh grade, which meant a new school and new teachers. He moved through the halls as if he were just visiting, never becoming a part of it. He carried Tiamat's tear with him wherever he went.

In October, his parents decided to have a party.

"An old-fashioned Halloween party," said his father, trying to inspire some enthusiasm in Jeremy. "We'll have a bonfire in the field, fresh cider, real costumes—no store-bought stuff allowed!"

Jeremy smiled grimly, and helped with the preparations. His father lit the bonfire with great ceremony, announcing they were celebrating a night when magic was let loose upon the world.

"It's beautiful, isn't it?" asked Mary Lou, walking up to stand beside him. She was dressed like a witch.

Jeremy shrugged. The leaping flames reminded him of Tiamat. It hurt to watch them.

Several other kids from school were at the party, too. Jeremy said hello to each of them, but not much else. His eyes were continually drawn back to the bonfire. As he watched the dancing flames he felt something struggling to break free inside him.

To his surprise, Miss Priest was at the party.

"Your mother invited me," she murmured, when she saw him at the refreshment table. "I hope you don't mind."

He shook his head numbly. But when he got a chance, he fled to the barn. Crawling into the stall where Tiamat had stayed, he pulled the diamond tear from his pocket and began to weep. His eyes burned, and his throat felt like it was on fire.

The weeping passed like a storm. Lying on the straw, he stared into the darkness, listening to the noises of the party outside. He was drifting off to sleep when a swirl of color flowed through his head.

Shivering, he sat up. Suddenly the nearly forgotten scar where Tiamat's tooth had pierced his palm began to throb. Sweat poured off his brow. He felt like someone had pounded a wedge into the back of his skull and was trying to lift off the top.

He clawed at the stall wall in a panic, until, suddenly, he understood what was happening. Tiamat was back!

"Ti?" he called. "Ti, where are you?"

Here! she whispered inside his head.

He spun around. She was nowhere in sight.

He turned again. *Where are you?* he thought desperately, terrified by the idea that he had lost the ability to see her.

Here, she repeated. *Right here with you.*

Finally he understood. She was not back in this world; she was still in her own world, where she belonged. But she was back inside his head.

Even better, he was inside *her* head. He was seeing through her eyes, feeling through her skin.

What he saw was a world filled with dragons.

What he felt was big.

We are big! announced Tiamat happily. Then she spread her wings—his wings—*their* wings, and threw herself from the edge of a cliff. Jeremy's heart lurched with fear. But the leathery wings caught an updraft, and with a sudden rush Tiamat began to soar upward.

Jeremy looked down from a dizzying height. The air was filled with dragons—great beasts of power and majesty, creatures with jeweled eyes and burnished skins. He caught another current of hot air in his wings and spiraled upward, looking out over a world of ferocious beauty. High volcanic mountains capped with plumes of smoke and ash were feeding fire to the sky. Dragons soared and wheeled above and between the mountains, spiraling up on

the currents of hot air that filled their leathery wings, like sparks spiraling up from a bonfire.

The world of the dragons.

Tiamat's world.

And now, suddenly, his world, too.

I missed you, he thought to Tiamat.

And I you, she replied. She said it in his mind, and she said it out loud, and when she spoke it was with a tongue of fire. Her flames curled through the sky, and in them he read the promise that he could return to this world every night. When he dreamed, he would dream of dragons. With Tiamat he would slither into jewel-studded caves, soar through ash-dark skies, and study ancient mysteries.

Fire in his eyes, Jeremy rejoined the party. When Miss Priest saw him she smiled. Reaching into her cape, she withdrew a ring and slipped it onto her left hand. In the light of the bonfire, Jeremy could see that the stone set in the ring's top was a tear-shaped diamond. He raised a questioning eyebrow, looking more like his father than he would have guessed.

Miss Priest smiled and nodded, and touched her lips with her finger. Then she turned and vanished into the night.

The next morning, Jeremy went to his desk. Humming contentedly, he arranged his pencils in front of him. Then he took out some paper—and began to draw.

A Note from the Author

"I desired dragons," J. R. R. Tolkien once wrote, and it seems he was not the only one. There is some powerful pull about these great creatures, something that sings to the imagination.

In one very real sense, I wrote about Jeremy and Tiamat because, like Professor Tolkien, I desired dragons. Yet I must confess that when I started the story, I had no idea how much dragon I was actually going to get. The truth is, I thought "The Dragon's Egg" (as I originally planned to call this tale) was going to be a short story. But I tend to get carried away—which is why *Jeremy Thatcher, Dragon Hatcher* ended up a novel.

I originally had the idea for this tale back in 1982, shortly after publishing *The Monster's Ring,* the first book to feature Mr. Elives' magic shop. I liked the store so much (basically, it's the magic shop I wanted to find when I was a kid myself) that I thought it would be fun to write other stories that sprang from a youngster buying one of Mr. Elives' unusual items. My plan was to make a book of such yarns, to be called *Tales from the Magic Shop.* Brainstorming one October afternoon, I came up with about a dozen things one might buy in the shop.

The thing is, every time I tried to write one of these ideas, it would get out of hand. Before I could finish the first version of "The Dragon's Egg," I could tell it was going to be much longer than I had intended. Still clinging to my first deluded notion, I started dividing it into chapters, thinking it could be the anchor story for the collection, maybe thirty or forty or fifty pages long.

But no, it insisted on being a book, or at least book length. And since I didn't have a publisher for it at that point, and had other books I was obligated to write, I set it aside. There it might have stayed—unfinished, unknown, and unloved—had not my friend Jane Yolen called one day to tell me Harcourt had engaged her to edit a new line of fantasy novels.

"If you could write a book like *The Monster's Ring* for me, that would be great," she said, little knowing that I was longing to return to the world of Mr. Elives' magic shop!

That this book has been as successful as it has is in no small part due to Jane's editorial pushing and advice. For example, the first version ended with Jeremy saying good-bye to Tiamat outside Mr. Elives' shop, instead of going behind the counter with her. And she was no bigger than a dog when she had to return to her own world—partly because I hadn't figured out how Jeremy could cope with her if she got any bigger. (No night flights for Jeremy in that version!) Jane wisely pushed me to do more. In the end, it took thirteen drafts to get to the book you are now holding.

Strange as it might seem, research was an important part of the process. I believe fantasy like this works best—feels more real—when it is grounded in folk tradition. Therefore, much of the dragon lore in this book comes from tales and stories told about dragons over the centuries. For example, while having Tiamat be invisible to everyone except Jeremy and Mary Lou was an easy solution to the problem of how to keep people from finding out about her when she got bigger (a problem I didn't have until the later drafts, obviously!), it was not until I found an old French tale with a dragon who was only visible to *some* people that I felt comfortable using it. The milk trick, too, comes from the old lore. Other things—such as the use of Tiamat's teeth and skin to create the door that would return her to the world of the dragons—were my own invention. That's part of the fun of doing something like this: building on what has come before.

Another part of the fun is finding out how many others there were like me—others who also desired dragons.

May your hearts take wing!